Lawson's Bluff

PEOPLE ARE TALKING ABOUT LAWSON'S BLUFF ...

I normally prefer stories about women. But you had me fully engulfed. You had the perfect mixture of mystery and a touch of a love story to keep my attention for the duration of the book. Excellent work!
—Sethany Hagel

I'm hooked ... started reading when we boarded in Montgomery—almost finished first six chapters. Wow. Jeff is such a great writer—sentences are packed with rich details and of course I'm eating up all the spiritual truths. So honored and thankful to have received this pre-copy. Finished it on the flight. Fabulous! Bravo Jeff.
—A.A. Salter

I'm half way through your book in one sitting. Couldn't put it down. Anxious to find some quiet time to finish it. You are indeed a gifted writer and you hold your reader in the palm of your hand.
—Lynn Breitenberg

Your skill as a writer had me feeling I was a fly on the wall.
—Sara Lowery Blackburn

LAWSON'S BLUFF

Jeff S. Barganier

ELK LAKE PUBLISHING INC.

PUBLISHING THE POSITIVE
Plymouth, Massachusetts

Cover and Interior Design: Derinda Babcock

Editor(s): Mel Hughes, Deb Haggerty

Author Represented By:

PUBLISHED BY: Elk Lake Publishing, Inc., 35 Dogwood Drive, Plymouth, MA 02360, 2021

Library Cataloging Data

Names: Barganier, Jeff S. (Jeff S. Barganier)

Lawson's Bluff / Jeff S. Barganier

216 p. 23cm × 15cm (9in × 6 in.)

ISBN-13: 978-1-64949-172-5 (paperback) | 978-1-64949-173-2 (trade paperback) | 978-1-64949-174-9 (trade hardcover) | 978-1-64949-175-6 (e-book)

Key Words: Alabama, hog hunting, romance, mystery, action/adventure, domestic terrorists, private security

Library of Congress Control Number: 2021934799 Fiction

DEDICATION

To MC, Ford and Bee: May you know the Lord and be free forever.

ACKNOWLEDGMENTS

Thanks to my publisher, Deb Haggerty, for making this book happen. Thanks to my editor, Mel Hughes, for making my words shine.

PROLOGUE

MUNICH: 1945

He maneuvered the jeep with care, surveying devastation as he patrolled the deserted sector. Allied bombing had been relentless. Church towers and eerie walls of a once-prosperous district poked from mountains of rubble. The soldier pulled over in front of the remains of a grand German mansion, cut the engine, and climbed out. He pulled a flashlight from his belt and entered through a gaping hole in its wall. A rat squealed in protest and scurried away. A huge red flag with black swastika hung down from the second-floor balcony in the cavernous foyer. Heavy marble-topped tables, tufted velvet sofas with carved legs, shredded brocade draperies, a toppled bronze bust were all covered in soot and debris. He stepped into an adjacent room, focusing his beam on a section of collapsed wall behind a large, ornate desk. Something once concealed had been exposed by the bombs, and the young sergeant's curiosity was piqued. In the gray bleakness of the room, his light revealed an impressionist splash of color that both surprised and excited his imagination.

CHAPTER ONE

PARIS: OCTOBER 2001

To the woman, he resembled a six-foot, two-hundred-pound Komodo dragon with beady eyes, swarthy skin and a long snout for devouring large prey ... like her. The only difference, she thought, was he stood on two legs like a man. As he struck her again, her legs gave way. She collapsed to the floor with a despairing howl and wondered if he would indeed devour her.

He stepped back and glared at her like a giant, venomous lizard about to devour a lamb. She scrambled up to make her escape, but another man burst into the room and blocked her.

He glared at her attacker and nodded toward the door. "Enough, Omar."

The first man left the room. She backed up and braced against the wall, hiding her battered face in her hands.

The man took a seat. "We have many ways of making you talk. A beating is the least of them. Do we need to use other methods?"

She didn't reply.

"Your husband is not cooperating."

"My husband doesn't know where the art is."

"He refuses to speak with us when we contact him."

"Does he know I'm alive?"

"Not yet. Why? Would it help us get the art if he knew that you are alive?"

"No. I told you. He doesn't know where it is. Only I know."

"How interesting. How old is your son now? Fourteen? Does he know where the art is?"

She looked up from her hands and stared at him through swollen eyes. "No one knows. Only I know."

"And you expect me to believe you?"

"I'm telling you the truth."

The man stared back at her. His eyes were dark and cold. "I could kill you right now if I wished. Or maybe sever your fingers, one at a time, and send them to your husband. I'll bet, that after receiving the first finger—the ring finger and ring—he would respond to us."

"Yes. I suspect he would. But if you kill me and/or sever my fingers, you will never have the art."

The man cocked his head to one side and observed her. "And why is that?"

"Because to retrieve the art you need me ... alive ... with my fingers."

The man slipped a switchblade from his pocket and pressed its jacket. A five-inch blade snapped out.

"I'm running out of patience."

She took a deep breath and let it out. "The art is in a Swiss bank vault. I put it there myself. Without my personal appearance and fingerprint scan, the art will remain there forever."

"So, you are my *L'argent Cle*, my key to money? We can just go get it?"

"No ..." she said. "Not yet, anyway."

CHAPTER TWO

ALABAMA: 2021

Journalist Carla Frederick leaned against the pickup's dusty passenger-side door, sweating, squirming, slapping mosquitoes. She had never set foot in a pickup truck. Born and raised in the San Francisco Bay area, she was also not accustomed to being around men like Jack Lawson. But her goal was to ensure everyone on the planet would soon know his name. Questioning the wisdom of accepting her assignment, she studied the interior of the dirty truck, making notes that would comprise the bombshell story she would email her editor in the morning. Alabama was, after all, a backward part of the country—the uncivilized South. She wiped red sweat from her brow and studied the dirty smear in her palm, wondered what the wet stuff was, then checked her lipstick in the mirror for the third time.

Carla knew that in Lawson's Bluff, Jack Lawson was respected as the kind of man who defended women, flew the flag, and would kill the enemy at the drop of a hat. Agile and fast, he was six-foot-four with a thick neck and chest, formidable biceps and Herculean legs. He could have played football for the NFL and fathered seven children by seven women. He wasn't that kind of man, but a simple man of integrity with an unusual passion— killing wild hogs.

His straightforward, polite manner impressed her. She noted he scarcely paid attention to her now, but not necessarily because she was unattractive or for lack of interest. She understood hunting wild hogs to be an intense, dangerous business—no place for a lady, at least not for one as inexperienced in the wild as she. She observed as he pushed his hat back against thick dark hair and scrutinized the sky through crystal-blue eyes. His leathery, bronzed-skin and muscular build testified to the serious potential of the man about to do business with brutes of nature. He looked like a Greek god in an Alabama ball cap, sleeveless sweatshirt, jeans, and wide alligator belt.

"Where did you get that belt?"

"I harvested it from a swamp not far from here." He smiled. "It has little to do with securing these jeans. Everything to do with securing Old Betsy." He patted the scabbard that held a gleaming, ten-inch, razor-sharp pig-sticker.

She grimaced. "So, tell me about this preserve, Jack."

"Sure. Lawson Preserve's three thousand acres stretch southwest along the Chubalatchee River. Its eastern border disappears into woods. The southern area contains mostly rangeland." He paused and studied the sky. "I figure the scout plane should be east of here over dense woods. The hogs—I call them feral aliens—tend to emerge from the middle of those eastern woods. They almost always do. And in greater numbers these days. There's a giant boar out there somewhere. He has one white ear and one black. I call him the Majority Leader. He's highly intelligent. Ghostlike. Eluded me for a long time. And another one I call Satan ..." In the truck bed behind them were well-padded cages holding two American-bred Catahoula leopard dogs, a giant black-mouth cur like Old Yeller, and a pit bull, all fitted with GPS collars. The sun dipped below the horizon, painting the sky orange against blue. Sufficient late-September daylight remained. "The eastern invaders will move about sundown, and become a little careless after dark," Jack whispered. The air cooled via a breeze stirring from the swamp, ushering in the sweet smell of freshly cut pines. "Smell that?" Jack asked.

"What?"

"The scent from the marsh. It's so peaceful out there," he said.

She noted the melancholy in his eyes. "Oh, yeah, I smell it now that you mention it."

Carla had peppered him with questions on the way out from the Lawson home place but became quiet and reserved in the wild. She was less fragile than Jack thought. Nevertheless, the savage land and uncertainty that lay ahead frightened her. She tried not to let it show. He was about to re-engage her in conversation when the dogs began howling and rocking the truck like the devil himself had descended upon them. She grabbed the door handle and pressed her feet against the floorboard as if she could slam on brakes and stop the chaos.

Neither she nor Jack noticed the dispassionate eyes of a monstrous hog watching them from a nearby thicket, analyzing and recording their activities.

Jack noticed her distress and smiled in amusement. "This is normal," he reassured her. "It'll soon be time to release these angels and see where their music will lead."

Jack had yet to break a sweat. He took a small round can from his back pocket and stuck some of its contents in his mouth. He grinned and offered her some. "No thanks," she smirked, dashing off a note. Jack shrugged, stuck the can back in his pocket, and resumed his sky watch. With a listening device in his ear, he waited for word from the pilot or other members of his team, Big O, Turnip, and Buck.

Jack stepped from the truck and surveyed the sandy road stretching south behind them. A huge black creature crossed the road a hundred yards away. "I've got a hog! Big one! Get on 'im, boys! I'm turning the dogs loose!" The dogs flew from their cages in mouth-foaming, teeth-glistening, growling, howling rage, like sparks from an uncontrolled fire, and vanished into the brush. Jack snatched the steering wheel, plowing earth, accelerating in the direction of the dogs. Carla braced herself and hung on for dear life. "This is where it gets exciting!" Jack shouted as they bounced along. "Fresh cur dogs are fast. They get ahead of the hog and he becomes slam worn out from the running confrontation. He just can't stand it. And he'll bay up. In other words, stop. At this point the hog is thinking, okay guys, I can't outrun you and you can't whip me. So, I'm going to stand here and tear you to pieces. Then the dogs just stand back and bark at him—sort of like treeing a coon or a bear. Big hogs are dangerous at this point!"

"Wonderful," she replied with a death grip on the door handle. "How big is the hog you saw?"

"I can't say precisely. Three, four hundred pounds, maybe. You might want to get your camera ready. Anything can happen now." The dogs' howling grew more distant. Jack tensed and listened to the chatter coming over the phone, interjecting instructions.

She nodded at the pit bull. "Why didn't you let that dog go, too?"

"I need him fresh for the kill!"

"What? I heard about hog-dog fights at a PETA meeting in San Francisco. But this is suicide! This poor little dog has to kill a four-hundred-pound hog all by himself?"

"Not exactly," Jack said, bringing the truck to a sliding stop. Seeing nothing, he checked the GPS monitor and spoke into the receiver. "They're bayed half a mile east of Old Swamp Trail close to Beaver Fork. I'm getting as close as possible then proceeding on foot!" Jack accelerated again for five hundred yards, and then he hit the brakes and steered sharp right onto a trail the truck barely fit. Limbs entered through the open window and whipped Carla's head and shoulders. She ducked toward the center of the cab. "Raise your window!" Jack shouted. He pushed the Ford forward, negotiating deep puddles and dodging trees, taking out smaller ones. Carla covered her head with her hands and grumbled. Jack howled like a fiend in league with his dogs.

They emerged from the heavy brush and bounced across an open field for several seconds before jerking back into thick underbrush. The dogs' howling seemed closer now. Carla had neglected Jack's advice and the tree limbs returned with a vengeance. She dropped against the seat. Her long blonde hair landed in Jack's lap. Peeping through her fingers, she realized she was millimeters from Jack's scabbard and Old Betsy. In consternation, she contemplated what she might do with Old Betsy if her editor was present.

"So, who's going to kill it? Is someone bringing a gun?" She yelled.

"I never carry a gun," he replied. Then Jack's hand appeared and patted the scabbard affectionately.

"You've got to be kidding me! That's barbaric! You're insane!" she screamed.

"Sorry, Carla. But it just makes it an even match. We're one hundred percent committed now. Once the hog is bayed, we have to go in fast or risk losing our dogs!"

Jack popped off instructions to his team members who were converging on the GPS coordinates from the north. Days of rain had saturated the earth, leaving the surface a soggy mess. Jack stopped a hundred yards from where the GPS indicated the dogs were located. He surveyed the woods for shaking foliage, but they saw nothing. Creeping darkness conspired to erase shadows and contrasts. But enough light remained to make their way on foot.

"You stay in the truck, Carla! I'll send one of the boys to get you once we're done with the hog."

"You're not leaving me here!"

"Stay in the truck. You'll be safe."

"I will not!" she shouted, clasping her camera. "I didn't come all the way from California to this hellish, uncivilized, southern wasteland to sit in a dirty, stinking truck. I'm here to get a story and photographs!"

Her bitter words affected Jack's mood. "You have good health insurance?" he asked in a cold voice.

"Yes. Why?"

"Just wondered." Jack snapped the cage release, freeing the pit bull. The animal flashed into the brush without so much as a yelp. It reached the fight in four seconds, scrambled through the underbrush and sank its teeth into the boar's right ear, becoming a tenacious fiend tethered to a tornado of flesh.

"Okay, let's go. Stay back and out of the way until things get quiet. Understand?"

"Got it!"

Jack sprinted toward the barking dogs, tramping through knee-deep water, dodging small trees and rocks. Within fifty yards, Jack spotted a stand of saplings quaking and snapping. The beast raged against the vicious hounds, spinning, charging, crashing through small trees and pulverizing underbrush. Jack hunched and approached the thicket in short, quick steps. Snarls, grunts, clacking of teeth, popping and cracking limbs, were all directly in front of him. But he still could not see the hog's position. Thick around the fray, underbrush and briars separated Jack from the fight and obstructed his view. The woods grew darker. A colossal rock jutted up through the thicket. Jack figured the hog had its back to the rock. But the hog used the rock as a killing wall. Trapped hounds fought for their lives. Blind with anger, the boar lashed out at the hounds, snapping its tusks and issuing its characteristic haw, haw, haw, haw, I'm mad and you're dead warning rally. It tossed one of Jack's prized Catahoula hounds above the brush, and the dog screeched in pain. Jack backed up and searched for a way to climb the rock for a better look. A waste of time. He watched in desperation. The hog airmailed the pit bull over the thicket. The dog rolled three times, regained its footing and disappeared back through the briars. Jack knew the pit bull was heading for the hog's ear, as trained. Jack guessed where the hog's tail was.

Carla was well behind, negotiating the same terrain, trying to maintain her footing in the wet muck. She stopped fifteen yards from the fight and steadied herself against a small tree, trembling, aghast at the hellish scene before her. The last eighty yards—wide open—had been an obstacle course, not a jog in Golden Gate Park. Her lungs burned from the sprint, and fear of the unknown dominated her mind. Her remaining stamina tapped strength from a mega-rush of adrenaline. Fighting queasiness, she raised her camera and clicked away ... the dog in the air ... the violent shaking of the trees ... Jack kicking a path into the thicket. She noticed other men approaching, one on a four-wheeler. Big O yelled out to Jack, but she couldn't fathom his Southern gibberish. She kept snapping movement.

Jack had to engage or lose his dogs. He kicked hard at the briars, trying to create an opening and see the hog's position. Spotting its hindquarters, he ripped through the thicket and into the fight. Thorns ripped his face, neck and arms.

Fueled by professional compunction to capture the action, Carla raced forward to where Turnip and Buck braced for whatever would happen next. Big O moved in behind Jack through the thicket. She slung her camera behind her back. "Help me up this rock!" she demanded. The men quickly obliged, giving her a hand up, then pushing her, scraping her hands and elbows raw and bloody. Reaching the top, she sprawled eight feet above the gory, chaotic stench below. She recovered her camera and continued to shoot.

The huge muscular creature resembled a short-legged bull. Instead of horns, it possessed five-inch, razor-sharp tusks that protruded from its long, foaming snout. Slits contained beady eyes, overlaid by blood and foam. The area below Carla looked like the aftermath of a twister—small trees shredded and trampled down. A mat of pulverized brush covered the ten-to-twelve square-foot death pit walled by dense brush. The severely wounded hound the hog had hooked and tossed lay against the far side of the pit. Another snarled directly in the boar's face but kept its distance. The black-mouth cur dog—the one Jack called Old Amos—had clamped teeth on the boar's left ear while the pit bull dangled from the other. Jack stood behind the beast, holding its powerful hind legs off the ground. At this, the boar stopped fighting the dogs and tried to plunge forward. It glared up at Carla as she snapped photos.

In one swift, athletic move, Jack twisted the boar's hind legs, then reached beneath it with his right hand, caught its front leg and threw the animal to its side, straddling it. Jack held tight the front leg, restraining the beast. Buck and Turnip burst through the bushes and helped Big O hold the hog down. Jack slipped Old Betsy from her scabbard, aimed for the heart, and drove the blade home.

Carla snapped another photograph and threw up.

The boys high-fived Jack. They made the traditional bet about the boar's weight. Then Jack turned his attention to inspecting and consoling his injured dog. "Hang on, boy." The other dogs were scratched up, too, but appeared to have no gaping wounds. Jack asked Turnip to get the wounded hound to the vet as soon as possible. Then he and the others chained the boar to the four-wheeler, pulled the carcass out of the thicket and readied it for transport to the nearest truck. As darkness enveloped the woods, the men strapped lights on their heads. Jack looked around. "Has anybody seen the reporter?"

"Up here," she answered weakly. Jack turned toward the rock and looked up. Carla was half prostrate and half dangling from its precipice, hair disheveled, face ashen and streaked with muck, arms bloody, vomit dripping from her chin and shirt. She stared down at Jack with uncertain, faint eyes. "I don't feel so good. Take the camera." She allowed the camera to slide by its cord down the face of the rock. Jack caught it and tied it to his belt.

"How'd you get up there?" he asked. Buck and Turnip laughed and went about their business.

"With their assistance. Help me down, please."

"Sure. Ease off in this direction. I've got you." Carla maneuvered toward the slope and slid—her blouse snagging sharp rock, dead limbs and thorn-covered vines—toward Jack's bloody hands. He caught her with a grin. She jerked away and tried to stand without help, but wobbly legs failed her.

Big O and the boys took the four-wheeler to haul the hog out to their truck on a makeshift gurney. So, Jack scooped Carla up in his arms and set out through the woods. "Thanks, boys! See you guys tomorrow. Good hunt," he said.

"Congratulations on number one thousand," they replied, grinning, watching him trudge away into the steaming blackness.

CHAPTER THREE

Jack hit the brakes hard, skidding to a stop. The hot night-mist emanated from the wet earth and enshrouded them. A vile odor filled the air. The dogs howled madly. "What are you doing?" Carla pleaded.

"It's the Majority Leader! There! See him?" Jack shouted. Carla struggled up from her slouching and peered through the windshield. A huge hairy boar with ten-inch tusks shook his head in anger and foamed at the mouth. His demonic eyes glowed red in the headlights. Half as big as the truck, it faced and challenged them. "I'm going to take him!" Jack yelled.

"Jack, no!" Carla clutched Jack's shirt, but she was too weak to hold him. He bounded from the truck. She watched in horror as Jack drew Old Betsy and raced toward the creature. She got out of the truck, slammed the door, and stood clinging to the mirror. Jack attacked the hog head-on, but the animal charged and gored Jack in the groin, flipping him in the air. Jack landed on his back in the road and the beast pounced on him, tearing him limb from limb. The hog obliterated Jack, leaving him a lumpy soup spread over the road. The Majority Leader turned from its mayhem and beamed its ember-eyes at the young woman. It stalked toward her with renewed purpose. She thought of letting the dogs go or getting back in the truck. Her legs shook like cornstalks in an earthquake. Fear incapacitated her. The leviathan continued toward her, closer, closer, popping its teeth ...

Someone banged on Carla's door. She jerked and sprang straight up in bed, aroused from the horrifying nightmare, drenched with sweat.

The door opened. "Miss Frederick? Are you up? Would you like some coffee?" the girl asked with a big smile.

"Uh, uh, oh, please, that would be nice. Black," Carla managed. "What time is it?"

"Twelve o'clock!"

"Pacific time?"

"No. Central standard time." The girl laughed. "It's only ten o'clock your time. I'll be right back."

"Oh. Okay. Wait. What day is this?"

"Saturday."

Carla stretched, waking up achy muscles. Stiff and sore from the previous evening's insanity, she wanted to get to work on her story, to meet a twelve o'clock deadline. Her original schedule called for leaving Lawson Preserve Sunday morning before the *Los Angeles World News* Sunday edition hit the streets. Now she rethought that schedule, seeing no reason to spend another night in Alabama. By the time the girl returned with coffee, Carla had downloaded photographs from her camera to her laptop and written the first line of her story:

> *Carla Frederick–Lawson's Bluff, Alabama.* Savagery is confined to the darkest realms of the earth, deep within the African bush or the unseen jungles of the Amazon's unexplored tributaries. Right? Think again. It's here, too, in America's southeastern interior where a rare breed of bloodthirsty men and their specially bred assault dogs stalk unwary, helpless animals and brutally murder them with their teeth, bare hands and knives. I've seen this gruesome business up close and personal. It's America, the not so beautiful ...

The girl knocked again.

"Come in."

She entered, carrying a tray with hot black coffee. "Thank you," Carla said, glancing up from her work. "Uh, have we met?"

"No. I wasn't here when you arrived yesterday. I was at a friend's party. I'm Dagny, Jack's sister. And you're a writer from LA. I've heard all about you. Oh, I would like to be a writer someday, too. And travel the whole world like you, Miss Frederick."

"Call me Carla," she said flatly, studying the young brunette beauty's innocent green eyes.

"Oh, thank you, Carla. That's wonderful. It's like we're long-lost friends. Gosh, you're all wet. Did you take a shower in that gown? I think Jack's in love with you. Oh, aren't you excited? You've come all the way from the West Coast to find love here at Lawson Preserve. That's so romantic."

"What?"

"Yes. I heard him say so last night when y'all came back from the hunt. They were helping you out of the truck. Daddy was mad. He thought Jack had let the hog get you. Sunama was wiping your face and trying to clean you up and get your mucky shoes off, you know, so you could come in the house. And Jack said ..."

"Slow down. Sunama?"

"Sunama is like our mother here at Brynhild. She raised me after Mama died. But not Jack. He's much older, you know."

"Oh. Okay. And Jack said ...?"

"He said: 'She's pretty tough, actually.'"

"Is that it?"

"Yes. But I could tell by the way he said it and the look in his eyes that he is in love with you." Carla pondered Dagny's words for a moment with amusement. At least, here is a female human being, and she's like the girls back home—talkative airheads. Of course, she's young too. But Carla had little time for distraction. "Okay. Well, I'm up against a deadline, Dagny. You'll have to excuse me. We can talk later. I need to finish my submission, or I'm in big trouble." She smiled.

"Oh, I so understand. I have an English teacher like that. Let me know if you need anything. I'll tell everyone you're not to be disturbed! We writers have to stick together," Dagny said, backing from the room. Carla smiled, gave Dagny a quick wave, took a gulp of coffee and continued typing:

> ... an America where men are beasts, too, only worse. Jack Lawson, heir to Lawson Preserve in Lawson's Bluff, Alabama, is one such man whose instincts seem governed by cold-blooded, flaming hormones and an unquenchable lust for blood.

Carla filed her story on time. She showered and dressed in jeans and a fashionable turquoise tunic. Then she packed her bag and went looking for someone to whom she could offer a farewell. She found Sunama in the spacious kitchen. "You're a little late for lunch with the family, Princess, but I've saved you a plate if you're hungry."

"Please, call me Carla. And"—it occurred to her—"yes, I'm starving. Thanks!"

Sunama was a large, red-headed woman with a gregarious nature and infectious smile. She snatched food from the refrigerator and set a place for Carla at the kitchen bar. Carla took a seat on a stool and wasted little time getting back into her journalistic mode. "So, Dagny tells me you landed the honor of cleaning me up last night. I am so sorry. But I remember your kindness. Thank you, Sunama."

"Oh, it was nothing at all, Princess. I hope you're feeling okay this morning. You got pretty scratched up on the hunt. The boys should have taken better care of you.

Hog hunting is a physical, dirty business. But I guess you have a job to do too. Girl! How did you end up covering a story like this?"

"My editor heard through the internet grapevine about some guy in Alabama who was about to kill his one-thousandth feral hog with nothing but a knife. He thought the story might generate a sensation in Los Angeles where people get animated about animal rights. You know—typical hunters stalk, maim, and kill animals with guns. So, the idea of this guy catching them with dogs and killing them with a knife sort of jarred his imagination, I guess. And, well, here I am. He may be revulsed when he reads my story and sees the pictures. We'll see. But tell me about you. Dagny says you raised her. What's your connection here at Lawson Preserve?"

Sunama turned from her dishes and beamed, her rosy cheeks accentuated by deep dimples. "My sweet Dagny. Well, her mama left us shortly after Dagny was born, and I needed work. I guess the rest is history." Sunama sighed.

Carla noted Sunama had said Mrs. Lawson *left*. "I'm not letting you off that easy. Tell me more. Where are you from? Are you related to the Lawsons?"

"Oh, in these parts, everyone is related somehow. But no, I'm an Oliver. My husband—they call him Big O—and me are local yokels. Our folks all worked at Lawson Mill for generations. The Lawsons subsidized the mill for twenty years, but they ran out of money and had to close. The mill created so many jobs for so many people ... but they had to shut her down." Sunama paused from her story and gazed out the kitchen window up at the red-brick mill standing atop the bluff across the river. "Them was the glory days for Lawson Mill. But they're gone now. I guess forever."

The dejection in Sunama's voice touched Carla. "So, how did you come to Lawson Preserve?" She asked the question with genuine interest.

"Well, like I said, I needed work. I never learned a trade, but I did help raise five little brothers and sisters. And Big O helped Mr. Lawson on the preserve and as a guide on hunts—they hunt everything here. White tail deer are still out there. But the hogs are taking over. So, years ago, I came out to help with little Dagny and never left. Big O and I never had children. We live in the little blue house down the road."

"Is Sunama your birth name?"

Sunama smiled proudly. "Oh, no. It's one of those names that children come up with when they're trying to learn to speak. My birth name is Suzanna. But little Dagny has always called me Sunama. I like the *ma* in it."

"I haven't had a chance to meet Jack's father. What's he like?"

"Mr. Lawson is a real nice man. He's the kind of man whose yes is yes and whose no is no. He'll give the shirt off his back to a man in need. But he don't like sluggards, now. He expects everybody to work hard and do right. It was his idea you stay here while working on your story. That's the way he is."

Carla shifted uncomfortably on the stool. "Oh, really? How nice. Did he ever remarry?"

"No, he never did. Hasn't even had lady friends over the years. I think, sometimes, that after Mrs. Lawson left, the land became his one and only. The land and caring for the land—it's in the Lawsons' blood. It's the same with most folks in these parts. I think that's why Jack hates them varmint hogs so bad. They disrespect the land so. They come here to kill, steal, and destroy, like those varmints that flew those planes ..." Sunama paused, as if embarrassed for rambling, then continued, "... and Jack's determined to stop them ... or die trying."

"Have hogs always been such a big problem?"

"Oh, no, ma'am. When I was a little girl, hogs were not a big deal at all. But over the years, they've multiplied like rabbits, and now, they're a major nuisance. The females drop two litters a year, 'round eight piglets a litter. About the only natural enemies they have is Jack, Big O, and the other boys in these woods that hunt. Every other creature in these woods, the hogs either eat or destroy their habitat."

Carla finished off a drumstick and grabbed another piece of fried chicken.

Jack walked in. "Good afternoon, Miss Frederick, Sunama."

"Is everyone in Alabama so formal? Please, 'Carla,'" she said, looking around to see who was there. Jack walked over and hugged Sunama.

"Sorry. It's just ingrained. We do it without thinking ... Carla. You clean up really well, by the way. I'm sorry we got you so messed up last night. Sure hope you're okay today. You apparently rested well." He chuckled. "Hog hunting the way we do it is pretty physical. I guess you know that by now, right?"

Carla studied Jack. His face was scratched up but clean-shaven, his dark hair combed. The ball cap was gone. He wore khakis, black golf shirt, and a brown buffalo belt that matched his clean boots. *Where's the redneck Jack Lawson from sixteen hours ago?*

His good looks and sharp clothes mesmerized her. As an unconscious reflex, she found herself patting her hair. Certain adjectives and characterizations in the story she had just submitted crossed her mind. During her writing, the hog fight was still fresh, with all its indignities. That vicious scene disturbed her mind's eye. But now, swimming in Jack's ocean-blue eyes, Carla sat confused and checked in her assumptions. She struggled to think of something to say—highly unusual for her. "Yes, well, it was quite an experience," she stumbled through. "That's for sure. But I covered an assignment in a Middle Eastern war zone last month. So, I'm not untested in the realm of the uncivilized. But the realm of the demonic? Now, that's another story altogether." She smiled, then grimaced, regretting the use of the word demonic, thinking it might have sounded too whacky or theological. She didn't wish to sound religious. Her spiritual beliefs were buried beneath a veneer, a symptom of her profession. Immersed in the seedy side of existence, she blamed God for the injustices in life.

"Okay, so we're uncivilized." Jack shrugged. "But your use of the word demonic tells me you understand hogs. You catch on fast. It is like a hellish war zone out there, and hogs are good metaphors for evil."

She didn't comprehend his reply because she was still thinking about her own untoward remark.

Jack stepped closer to Carla, returning her gaze, and spoke in a calm, serious, tone. "Would you say that last night was similar to your Middle Eastern experience, Carla?"

She reflected on the question for a moment and then answered in a slow, sober tone. "Well, fear was an element both times. Struggle was also present. But over there, in the Middle East, it was man against man, brother against brother. Last night it was man against beast, beast against beast, man and beast against beast. Over there, everyone had guns. Last night, no one had guns. Or did the hog have a gun? Oh, I don't want to speculate. You had a knife. I do remember that. And I guess I was the only woman within ten miles on both freaking occasions. I remember thinking that."

Sunama turned from the sink and stared at Carla, wide-eyed. "Honey, you need rest!"

Carla and Jack both studied Sunama with amusement, then Carla took a breath and continued with her drama. "Over there, I stood atop a hotel and filmed and wrote about action happening mere blocks away. I felt the crack of automatic weapons in my bones. Last night, I sprawled on a rock, only feet from the action and saturated in it. It's less nauseating when you see carnage from a great distance. That's for sure. Last night was too close, too personal."

Silence dominated the air for a moment following Carla's answer. Sunama shook her head like a mother concerned about her child's health. She dried her hands and left the room. Jack smiled. "How about I show you the sights and sounds of Lawson's Bluff this afternoon, if you're not too busy? It is Saturday, after all, and a beautiful day in Alabama. We'll be eating late by the pool. That gives us the rest of the afternoon. If you would like to, that is. Maybe you'll find material for a new story," Jack said.

Sunama spoke up from just inside the adjoining room where she had paused to eavesdrop. "Just go with it, baby. Make Jack buy you something pretty. After last night, you deserve to be pampered."

Jack and Carla laughed.

Jack's invitation surprised her. She contemplated the offer. He was dressed decently. The knife was gone. *Away somewhere being sharpened?* "Hmm, I did bypass town on the way in. Sure, okay, why not?"

"Great. I think Lawson's Bluff will surprise you. Of course, the town's little more than a main street flanked by red-brick two-story buildings. It's nothing like LA."

"Tell me more."

"Well, today, little shops fill street-level spaces. Some of the upper floors have been converted to residential where artists and professionals live and work."

"Sounds interesting."

"There are a few streets perpendicular to Main Street. Mostly single-family homes and at least one bed-and-breakfast mansion. The nearest franchise is miles away. You won't see any big box stores in Lawson's Bluff. But we have a historic hardware store still thriving."

"That's cool. I want to visit," she said, clapping her hands. "Were you Lawsons around back then?"

"Oh yeah. Lawsons were a big part of the town's development. They laid it out in the shape of a cross. But that's hard to see now that lots of other streets connect to Main. You can stand on the front steps of Lawson Mill, peer up Main Street, and behold the front of a small white chapel. My great-great-grandfather helped erect that chapel with his own hands."

"Jack, you're making me curious. Sounds so interesting and beautiful."

"There's more." He smiled. "The crowning distinction of Lawson's Bluff, apart from its striking white chapel and scenic mill overlooking the river, is the unusual roundabout located at the midway point of Main Street, showing the creative thinking of the original designers of the village." Jack made a circle with his hands and arms. "This roundabout was once the site of a stone monument commemorating the Ten Commandments."

"You Alabamians and all your Ten Commandments monuments." She smirked.

"Don't get ahead of me now."

"Sorry."

"But they yanked up and relocated the stone to the chapel grounds around the turn of the twenty-first century. In its place, the people erected an elaborate monument featuring a giant boar leaping forward in great travail with dogs in hot pursuit. The citizens of Lawson's Bluff transformed the curse of feral hogs into gold.

"More recently, my Dad led the movement to convert the abandoned mill into a thriving market for fresh local produce, trendy restaurants, arts, crafts, boutiques. Today, it's a country mall, attracting shoppers from all over. Lawson's Bluff is growing for the first time in a century and a half, bolstered by visitors who come to shop, trout fish and hunt large game on Lawson Preserve. The population has tripled. But the town's still a well-kept secret, a little economic Shangri-La in the backwoods where razorbacks roam and sturdy men sharpen their knives against invaders they despise but have come to appreciate. Some of those guys, like me, are in demand for their hunting skills—as guides. So, there you have it. End of lecture."

Carla clapped again. "Wonderful. I can't wait. When do we leave?"

CHAPTER FOUR

Jack escorted her to the passenger side of the SUV and opened the door. She smiled and looked askance at him. "Thank you."

"Of course. And, please, don't look so surprised," he said, a trace of hurt in his voice.

"You have to admit—bit of a contrast to yesterday."

Jack grinned. "*Yesterday*, we hunted wild boar. In that world, the rules are different. They have to be." She stepped in. Jack closed her door, walked to the driver's side and climbed in. Her eyes never left him.

"Point accepted. I like being treated like a lady. It feels nice for a change. The guys I work with are not always so respectful. But, then again, the media business is sometimes like hunting hogs." She laughed. They eased down a winding road past the preserve's private airfield, hanger, some maintenance outbuildings, and Sunama's home. The road hugged the river for half a mile, leading to an old covered bridge. Jack turned onto the bridge and eased along, giving Carla a chance to view the shimmering water below. Bright yellow trees shaded its entrance and exit. "What wonderful trees! I love ginkgo trees. And look at that river. How beautiful."

"I thought you might enjoy crossing here. My preferred route to town. Mother planted these ginkgoes. She loved to come here in the fall and collect their brilliant yellow leaves for various projects."

"It's all breathtaking. Can we stop? I'd like to snap some photos."

"Sure." Jack stopped, lowered the windows and killed the engine. The rushing water below them gurgled and splashed over the rocks.

Satan's dispassionate eyes watched them from a distance.

"Oh, this is so amazing," Carla said, fiddling with the lens cap. "Postcard perfect. And the air is so crisp and cool. The sky so blue." She wanted to ask about his mother but felt uncomfortable going there. She had other questions, too. Jack eased from the covered bridge and headed north along a narrow country lane toward the village.

"You're not using tobacco today?"

"I don't use tobacco." He smiled.

"But yesterday you did. Remember? On the hunt? You offered me a plug. Isn't that what it's called—a plug?"

"I suppose. But I didn't offer you tobacco. It was dried spinach. I carry a container of it when I hunt. It's a good source of vitamins and I love the taste. Say, you jump to conclusions."

"Spinach?" she asked in disbelief.

"Yep."

"How was I supposed to know it was spinach?"

"By asking."

"Wow. My preliminary research appears to have let me down." She laughed.

"How's that?"

"My research indicated all respectable hunters in the South chew tobacco—*Red Man*, to be exact."

He grinned. "Well, many do. But I don't want my chin surgically removed due to cancer. So, I dip spinach."

"I like spinach, too."

"Well, I'll remember to offer you some on our next hunt."

"Our next hunt? That's a bit presumptuous, don't you think?"

"It's an invitation. You haven't lived until you've taken your first hog."

She rolled her eyes. "I'll think about that until a certain place freezes over."

They ascended a hill and homes appeared. Jack turned left on Main Street and parked in the first empty space. He stepped from the Rover and quickly walked to the other side, but Carla was already getting out.

She noticed his approach. "Oops. Sorry. I forgot the rules."

"My bad. Too slow. I'll leap over the hood next time."

Carla laughed. "I wouldn't be the least surprised!"

Birds serenaded them from small oaks that lined the colorful sidewalks of Main Street.

"This is gorgeous, Jack." She pointed at the shops. "The shops have pots of flowers out. And look at the colorful pavers in the sidewalk. How unique."

"And no parking meters," Jack said. "That's what I like. And see the lamp posts with banners? *Lawson's Bluff. Founded 1816.* And the town's logo—dogs chasing a hog?"

"Is that coffee I smell?"

"Want a cup?" Jack asked.

She held Jack's gaze for a moment and smiled. "Maybe later?" Taking a deep breath of the aroma, she raised her camera and snapped photos with abandon.

An occasional hunter passed, dressed in camouflage. She studied them. Some carried knives. "Except for the knives, this reminds me of quaint towns in Oregon I like to visit. I'm truly impressed." She smiled and nodded.

"Thanks. That's what we like to hear. Our town council studied other towns our size and worked to give ours an ambience that would attract visitors and cottage-type firms."

"They've done a really nice job," Carla said with genuine enthusiasm.

"An astonishing contrast to what you've witnessed until now, huh?"

"Yes. Of course. I mean, the oddity of such picturesque beauty emerging from this violent wilderness. Civility— there's that word again—co-existing with barbarism. Alabama's a paradox." She lowered her camera and looked into Jack's eyes. "I kind of feel the same way about you, Jack. If I were meeting you now for the first time, my perspective would be quite different. But having witnessed the terrible violence you're capable of ... you're an incongruity, too."

Jack smiled. "You're beginning to admit there might be another side to this story. That's what I think."

She feigned distraction, gazing toward the old mill high on the bluff then looking north to the gleaming white chapel. She pointed. "The monument?"

"Yep. Replaced the Ten Commandments. It's a tribute to Catahoula hounds, hunting dogs like mine. Let's visit the mill. Then we'll walk down to the monument and up to the chapel. How does that sound?" They passed shops, pausing to look in windows, and sauntered toward Lawson Mill.

The mill's entrance was adorned by huge black and white photographs depicting its glory days. Jack pointed to a photograph of the mill's workers gathered on its steps. "That's my great-grandfather on the front row. He was working as a common laborer like everyone else. But he ended up managing the mill until he died in his late seventies. His father built the chapel. I imagine he may have helped, too."

"You favor him a little bit, I think," Carla said. She studied Jack, then the picture. "You have his prominent chin, high cheekbones, a hint of a Roman nose, uh, something about his eyebrows. They protrude slightly," she said, examining Jack's. "I wonder if his eyes were blue."

"My grandfather told me there was a strong resemblance."

"Did you have a relationship with your grandfather?"

"I remember him well. Unfortunately, I was just a kid when he died. So, time ran out on our budding relationship. But I remember overhearing an interesting family legend about him."

"What?"

"That he fought in World War II and brought home a treasure he found in Germany. But if he did, I've never seen it. Nothing to it, I guess."

"Interesting. So, your roots run deep here," she said with a trace of jealousy.

"Yeah. Lawsons go back many generations. We have a lot of blood, sweat and tears in this land. My forefathers helped tame this country, you might say."

Carla thought for a moment about his use of the word tame. "So, how does your keen sense of ancestry affect you, Jack?"

"Good question. I'd have to say it's like the ballast of a ship. The knowledge of my ancestors, what they went through for me, what they left behind, the freedom they secured for me—all that steadies me and gives me a sense of responsibility to stay upright. Lawsons have fought in every war this country has been in. Lawson men are buried on three continents. How about you? Are you in touch with your roots?"

Jack's eyes searched Carla's face. She hoped it looked better with makeup replacing the muck and vomit. But the question surprised her. She stopped and thought for a moment before answering. "My roots? Umm, you know, I can't say. I've never seen pictures of my ancestors, not like these. I'll have to ask Dad next time I'm in Virginia. That's where he lives. Mom's in San Francisco. They married late in life. Had me. Divorced not many years afterward. My grandparents died when I was a little girl. Talk of blood, sweat, tears, things left behind, freedom—that's all a little foreign to my experience, I guess."

"Well, family is pretty important in this part of the country. Do you ever have thoughts of settling down and starting a family?"

She blinked several times but couldn't find words. *It wasn't exactly a proposal.*

He shuffled his feet and suppressed a smile. "You okay?" he asked.

"Excuse me? I mean ... may I be excused? I mean ... is there a lady's room?"

Jack straightened and looked around. "Sure, around the corner on the left."

"Thanks. I'll be back." His eyes were back on her as she turned to dash away.

In the restroom, Carla dialed her boss, Arlan Anderson, at the *World News*. He answered on the first ring. "Arlan, this is Carla. I need you to hold my story on Jack Lawson. Don't run it. Not yet, anyway. I need more time."

CHAPTER FIVE

"Hold the story? No can-do, baby. You've written a blockbuster! The whole building has read it. You've created a firestorm here. It's been partially leaked to the street already. And the photographs! Are you freaking kidding me? These will end up all over the net. They're un-freaking-believable! Our readers are going to flip out. This will win you an award, maybe even a raise!"

"Arlan! You don't understand. There are some, let's say, nuances I need to work out. And parts of the story are not completely accurate."

"Since when is accuracy important? Just kidding. So, okay, like what?" Anderson snapped.

"Well, like the part about 'the ritual chewing of tobacco inflaming Jack Lawson's cold-blooded hormones.' He wasn't even chewing tobacco. It was spinach!"

Anderson laughed like a maniac. "What? Did you say spinach? That's hilarious. Do we have a Popeye-redneck-pig-killer on our hands?"

"Yes! I mean ... no! And stop laughing. It's not funny. I have a professional interest in getting this story right. And I'm discovering there may be an even bigger story here. I need more time."

"Look. Tobacco, spinach, whatever his fancy. Makes no difference to me. The story's sensational. It'll be front page tomorrow. Your amazing photographs will sell papers! Selling papers pays salaries. I like getting a salary."

"Arlan!"

"Sorry, baby. Tell you what. Stay out there and work on that bigger story if you like. Take some time off. You've been working hard lately. Keep in touch. Gotta go." Anderson hung up.

She knew calling him back was an exercise in futility. He wouldn't answer. "You jerk!" Carla stomped her foot and froze for a moment. Her story stampeded through her brain. She shut her eyes tightly and grimaced, recalling the more strident lines and visualizing the more gruesome photographs Arlan was sure to publish. She stepped from the restroom to find Jack waiting.

"You ready to see the mill?"

Carla shrugged. "Sure. So, Jack, where does one get a knife like Old Betsy?"

"I had mine custom-made by a guy near Double Springs, Alabama. Why do you ask?"

"Oh, I was just wondering."

They eased along and Jack introduced Carla to friends and merchants who warmly greeted her, perhaps thinking she was there to write glowing reports about Lawson's Bluff and its people. She received their accolades with a stitch of guilt. More than a few attractive young women tried to corner Jack, but he politely evaded them. They strolled through the renovated mill with all its quaint shops, taking in the fabulous views of the river, and then walked back out to Main Street and toward the other end of town. When they reached the roundabout, Carla snapped a few pictures, including one of Jack standing in front of the monument. She stood and studied the statue of the hog and dogs, and then she turned to Jack with a perplexed look. "So, Jack, make me understand the culture here. It seems so bizarre—this infatuation with hogs and dogs and violence and slaughter. It's like being on the set of a sci-fi movie."

Jack nodded. "It's like this. For ninety-nine percent of the people in Lawson's Bluff, there is little or no infatuation with hogs and dogs and violence. For them, life has everything to do with economic survival, entrepreneurship, free enterprise, individual initiative, pride, that sort of thing. Some of our residents are newcomers, attracted to the beauty and community. They just go with the flow. Then there are the people who grew up here, the descendants of families who worked at Lawson Mill for decades. When textile production began to shift overseas, my grandfather and father tried their best to keep the mill going and preserve the livelihoods of our people. But it became impossible to compete against Chinese slave labor and subsidized foreign industry. We were forced to close.

"Meanwhile, the feral hog population exploded. We realized we could possibly solve two problems. First, bring hunters in from outside to help us reduce the number of insatiable hogs that destroy everything in their path, and second, reinvent our town as a haven for hunting, outdoor recreation, and tourism. We have some of the best trout fishing in the Southeast within minutes of here. If you want to harvest an alligator for a new pair of boots, we have the gators and a first-rate boot-maker who can custom-design and make you a pair. If you want to kill or catch a wild hog or deer for a trophy or to fill your freezer, we can make it happen. The hog theme you see repeated is merely that, a theme around which we build commerce and opportunity. We are playing the hand we were dealt. As for the other one percent—you may include me in that group—it has a lot to do with the hogs and dogs and violence and slaughter.

"The hogs I harvest go to good use. Many of them are sent to processors and the meat donated to various charities or supplied to fundraising events. But my personal goal is to rid Alabama of feral hogs forever. And maybe, by the time I have accomplished that lofty goal,

America will have fully transitioned—that is, come to its senses. Manufacturing will have returned to towns like Lawson's Bluff, and free people will once again make goods for consumption by free people. And American politicians will no longer advance slavery in dictatorships around the world to line their own pockets."

"Are you saying you vent your political frustrations by killing hogs? Because that sounds a little strange," Carla said.

"No, not exactly. I assure you there are easier and better ways to vent political frustrations than by hunting hogs," Jack said sternly.

"Such as?"

"One could run for Congress, for example. But that would mean becoming a compromiser. Who wants to compromise? Killing hogs is so much more accurate and definitive." He laughed. "On the other hand, failing to be involved in the political process in America is like being in open rebellion against our constitutional republic which is supposed to be of the people. In any event, I kill hogs because fighting evil, however it may manifest, is a noble cause."

"Fighting evil is a noble cause?" Carla repeated. "Now I'm really confused. Jack, you make it sound like a fairy tale. What on earth does killing hogs have to do with fighting evil?"

Jack smiled. "To understand the relationship of killing hogs to fighting evil, you have to have a certain world view—the Jack Lawson world view, that is. First, you have to recognize that evil does, in fact, exist. Second, you must believe that evil is capable of existing in and utilizing nature. And third, you have to believe that to allow evil to inhabit the natural realm without opposition is to abandon truth. Jesus once sent a bunch of demonic pigs off a cliff. Well, they're back."

Carla's face contorted as she struggled to follow Jack's strange logic. "What? Are you teasing me?" *Maybe he's only half kidding. Is this a philosophy test?* She walked over to a bench and took a seat. Jack followed, and they sat facing each other.

"Not at all," Jack continued. "Do you recognize that evil exists?"

"Well, of course."

"And how do you define evil?"

"Evil is bad, wrong," Carla said, gesturing for emphasis.

"Says who?"

"Says every sane person." She chuckled.

"And who gets to say who is sane and who is insane?"

"Psychiatry, I guess."

"So, if psychiatry says, for example, that pedophilia is normal, does that settle the question? Should the government include pedophilia as a protected class of people and thus sanction the sexual abuse of children?"

"Of course not!"

"Well then, are you saying that pedophilia is evil and should be prohibited?" Jack asked.

Carla thought about it. "I guess I am. Sure. I am."

"Then do you believe that sexual abuse of children is always wrong? Do you believe it is absolutely wrong under all circumstances?"

"I ... I can't think of any valid purpose for sexually abusing children. It's all about the sexual gratification of adults who commit those acts."

"I agree. So, in your opinion, if adults engage in the sexual abuse of children, are they setting themselves in opposition to absolute truth, that is, are they engaging in conduct that is in every respect evil?"

Carla gave it some thought. "Well, yes."

"And would you also agree that if society fails to restrain the evil of pedophilia, that failure would constitute a de facto abandonment of absolute truth?"

"I guess. But I still don't see what all of this has to do with hogs."

Jack leaned slightly toward Carla.

Her eyes grew wide as she wondered what strange thing he would say next.

"Carla, if one fails to oppose evil, is that person advancing evil and abandoning absolute truth?"

Carla stared at Jack. *This is a very complex hog hunter.*

"Take your time."

"So, you're saying that feral hogs are pedophiles and must be stopped at all costs?"

Jack laughed out loud. Carla laughed with him. He relaxed on the bench. "No, ma'am. I just love to hunt. And feral hogs, like their human protégés—politicians who turn a blind eye to evil—are destroying my country, my land, its creatures, its beauty, and everything good and decent that our forefathers passed on to us to care for and protect, so that, someday, we might pass this heritage on to our children. You see, I believe when a nation turns its back on truth, evil forces are unleashed. I believe the reason we are seeing so many wars and rumor of wars, for example, is because demonic forces are having a heyday in the realm of human relations. Truth has been abandoned via political correctness in the West. The West doesn't even recognize evil anymore. This emboldens those forces. And now they're congregating here, on our land, in an attempt to destroy us from within. Among others, they've taken the form of feral hogs. Remember, you said yourself that in the Middle East you witnessed brothers fighting brothers, creating massive human suffering there. Why? And look at the geophysical realm: earthquakes, superstorms, tsunamis, throughout the world, now more frequent than at any time in recorded history."

"But can't all of that be explained by climate change?" Carla asked.

"Does climate change cause evil? Or does evil cause climate change? Just asking. I would argue it's not gases from the human body or methane from cows or garbage dumps that causes evil to flourish. Rather, it's the condition of human hearts, the turning away from the Creator of the Universe, the Truth. When we stop embracing Truth, evil reigns. Well before Pontius Pilate, who was trying to be politically correct, asked Jesus, 'What is truth?' the battle has raged. In my view, feral hogs personify evil. They don't see themselves as evil, of course. They just do what swine do—like the Nazis did what they did to the Jews, like smallpox does what smallpox does, like plague germs do their thing, like terrorists do their murdering. Feral hogs are a form of pestilence, too, a pestilence we visit upon ourselves because we have abandoned timeless absolute truths. Did you know in Washington, DC, it's against the law to kill rats? Rats must, by law, be relocated *with their families* to safe zones, not exterminated. By the way, it's my understanding a certain prominent psychiatric association has pronounced pedophilia is normal."

Carla stared at Jack in disbelief. "Tell me you're kidding."

"I'm not. So, Carla, to me, disease-carrying wild hogs, not unlike disease-carrying rats, are like our enemies. They come here intent on destroying our republic. It makes no difference to me that they're not human and don't know right from wrong. Like our human enemies, who apparently have lost all sense of right and wrong, they have no respect for us or our sovereignty, our borders or laws. They violate our property, kill our wildlife, do billions in damage to our crops. They eat baby deer, birds, cute bunny rabbits, snakes, and humans if they stand still long enough. In fact, it has been reported they have attacked, killed, and devoured sick and feeble migrants attempting to walk into the United States from Mexico. Hogs are smart and ravenous. When they run out of other creatures to ravage, they turn on each other. They'll even devour their young—which makes them almost ... human. They're super-evasive and hard to hunt. That's why I use dogs, by the way. Hogs are hard to hunt with guns or bows. They have poor sight but keen hearing. I've seen twenty hogs scatter to the four winds when a hunter simply clicked his safety off." Jack paused and studied the sky as if his next thought might be there.

Carla was still a bit cynical but amazed at Jack's depth. But who in her world could even relate to Jack? His hog hunting could be seen on the surface. But below the surface was a gigantic iceberg story of pain, struggle, honor, religious convictions, perceived oppression and resistance, real men, and issues she had never thought about. Jack was an enigma to her—but an interesting enigma.

"Our sovereignty, our laws. Wow, Jack, you're really deep for a red ..." Carla stopped.

"For a redneck?"

"Sorry, I didn't ..."

"Sure you did. You're here to do what members of the biased, anti-American press do so well. Write a story. Create a legend. Then, when the facts and truth eventually come out, when it's too late to correct the record, ignore them. I'm trying to give you a real story. But it's not the one you came for. The hunt you experienced yesterday is not the whole story. There is some science and reason behind what I do, how I do it, and why I do it. It's not all bloodlust. I'm the guy who has caught a thousand hogs, remember?"

I know all too well. He was right in many respects, and when her story hit the front page of the *World News* in the morning, he would be vindicated and would probably despise her. The sun dropped behind the buildings. She shivered, rubbed her arms, and looked away in confusion. He gave her an apologetic smile.

"I'm sorry. That was uncalled for. Wait here. I'll be right back."

Jack walked across the street and disappeared into a shop. He returned with a University of Alabama sweatshirt and two cups of hot chocolate. "Here's a souvenir for you and some hot chocolate to warm you up," he said. Jack handed her the colorful shirt.

She smiled at him and pulled it on. "Thank you, Jack. So thoughtful. I think I hear what you're saying. I certainly have not heard any of this before now. You've definitely given me a broader perspective on the subject of hog hunting, one that I never in my wildest dreams would have come up with on my own."

"Carla, look around you." Jack waved his hand in an arc. "You see these people going about their business in perfect harmony? They're simple folks. But they understand what's important, what's real, what's valuable. They have faith in something beyond themselves. They believe in the Living Truth, someone who gives them courage to face their problems. You won't find these people flying planes into buildings. They don't get too hung up on the prevailing winds of political correctness either. Don't they look civilized to you? Hey, look at that guy over there." Jack pointed to an older man who eased down the sidewalk with a shotgun slung over his shoulder. "Look. He's carrying a gun. Nobody's concerned. Nobody even notices. What would happen if he were in California?"

Carla looked away, then at her watch.

"Sorry. We Southerners just get tired of the double standards and ignorance. Tell our story honestly. That's all I ask. And tell the whole story." He smiled. "Let's walk."

They continued their stroll toward the chapel. At the top of the long series of steps up to the petite, wooden building, Carla turned and took a photograph of the town stretching back to the mill. The sun spilled over tree tops and between buildings, and the town was sparkling, bathed in late-afternoon sun and light spilling from shops. The warmth of the sun on her face relaxed her, and she leaned against one of the chapel's four columns, soaking up the moment. She took a deep breath and exhaled. "This is beautiful. I must admit, I had reservations about coming here. I visualized something else entirely. Thanks for bringing me. You've deconstructed my bigoted views about the South. That's, by the way, what an English teacher told me as a freshman my first day in her class. She said, 'we are going to deconstruct your bigoted views about what writing is.'"

Jack nodded and then sighed. "Thanks for listening. You've deconstructed my bigoted views about journalists." He smiled. "When do you leave?"

"I have a flight out tomorrow morning from Birmingham. Why?" She asked, searching his eyes.

"I was thinking—you know, you just got here. There's a lot you should see. Why don't you spend a few days with us? If you will, I promise not to talk about hogs or politics at all."

"A few days?" But seeing he was quite serious, she continued, "Oh, thanks, Jack. I don't know. I've got a busy schedule, and you all have business to attend to as well."

"Business can wait. At least delay your flight. Leave Monday. Stay one more day. We can come here for church in the morning and eat lunch afterwards at the little restaurant at the mill. And you need to try fly-fishing. I know the perfect place."

Her eyes moistened.

"What's wrong? Did I say something?" Jack asked.

"I need to sit down."

"Sure. Let's go inside."

"Can we do that?"

"Yeah. These doors are never locked."

The doors made a crunching noise as he pushed on the left door and pulled the right door open. They stepped inside and took seats on a pew.

She sat still for a few moments, taking in the simple interior. "It's so serene. Wow, the perfect place for confessions."

"What do you mean?" Jack asked.

Carla lowered her face into her hands. "Jack, I've already filed the story. I emailed it this morning to my editor. He loved it. And it's not pretty—which is why he loved it. It's the perfect piece of yellow journalism to sell papers. When we were up at the mill and I went to the restroom, I called him and tried to get him to hold it, but he refused. In his words, I've already created a firestorm."

"Is that all?" Jack asked.

She looked up. "Isn't that enough?"

"That's hilarious. I can't wait to read it."

"You're not angry?"

"No," he shrugged. "I may have been if you had run off—and then I read it and thought you intended to hurt us. But I can understand how you may have written some things hastily and sent them off. That's okay. No, I'm not going to allow a little yellow journalism to bother me. Can I read it tonight?"

Carla looked desperate.

"Just kidding."

"I feel bad about it now, Jack. I woke up this morning in a lurch after a horrible night's sleep. I had two hours to meet my deadline. I was frantic and still traumatized by the hunt. I was irritable. I knew what they wanted, and I delivered without any concern as to how my words would affect you, your family, your reputation, or this town. After all, I hardly knew you or anything about you or your family. Had I left earlier today, before you invited me to visit Lawson's Bluff, I would have never seen you again. I would have been happy to have allowed the chips to fall where they might, regardless of who got hurt. I'm truly ashamed. I've been unprofessional. I think I've learned a lesson. But, oh, Jack, what I wrote is so acidic and condescending—stuff like flaming hormones ... PETA's worst nightmare ..."

"I beg your pardon?" Jack smiled.

Carla choked and clutched her chest as if lamenting her greatest blunder in life. "They're going to crucify you, Jack. The horrible, deranged photographs, cold-blooded, flaming hormones ..." she repeated. Then she commenced laughing.

She didn't quite know why. But it felt good. As far as she was concerned, it was okay to laugh. An older couple meandered in. They seemed annoyed. Frivolity must have seemed inappropriate to them in the chapel's reverent environment. Jack and Carla tried to suppress their laughter but could not.

"It's our cold-blooded, flaming hormones," Jack quipped, sending Carla to the floor in guffaws. The visiting couple stiffened and departed.

"The Bible says that laughter's as good as medicine," Jack said.

"It works for me. I haven't had such a good laugh in a long time." Carla dried her eyes on her new sweatshirt.

They settled down again and observed the interior of the old chapel. The walls were whitewashed planks. The stained-wood ceiling was the mere underside of the steep roof, kept aloft by cross-support and V-shaped beams. Period light fixtures with candles hung from the beams and candles sat in holders along the walls. The windows had inside shutters. They were open. Sun-setting light infused a golden glow roundabout Jack and Carla. The floor was burnished-by-age, wide-plank pine that had been harvested from Lawson Preserve almost two centuries before. It seemed unchanged by time.

"I used to love coming here with my grandfather—we called him Pop—when I was little. We sat right up there," Jack pointed, "at the front. Pop always sat on the end. I sat beside him. Grammy on my left. Mom and Dad to the left of her. That was back in the day when Reagan stood at the Brandenburg Gate and challenged Gorbachev to open the gate and tear down the wall. He instinctively understood that evil must be confronted, whatever the cost. Those were the days just before the feral hog population exploded. Reagan's passing seemed to usher in a new breed of feral politicians, too, who would side even with our enemies." Jack stared straight ahead, deep in thought, his promise to avoid such talk already broken.

Without thinking, Carla placed her hand on Jack's shoulder and rubbed. She saw agony in him. "You are truly a mysterious character. One day you're Tarzan running through the jungle, slaying wild beasts, catching maidens in distress. The next day, you're Churchill's ghost, pontificating on the state of the world. Who are you, Jack Lawson?"

"Won't you stay another day or two? Nobody in Lawson's Bluff reads the *World News*. You're safe here."

"I might." She smiled.

Jack checked his watch. "We should be getting back to the house. I can't miss my own birthday party."

"Birthday party?"

Within a hundred yards of the house, Jack lowered the front windows and slowed to a crawl. Cars and pickup trucks covered the yard. The mansion glowed with light. Torches blazed around the pool area. They smelled the unmistakable aroma of meat cooking and heard music and dozens of people laughing and talking. "Wow! Some party! Is all this for you?" Carla gushed.

"I reckon so."

"Jack, I'm not dressed. I didn't really bring anything proper for a party."

"You're fine. In that Alabama sweatshirt, you'll fit right in."

Albert Lawson was a distinguished-looking man of medium build, straight as a board and a picture of health. Jack was a few inches taller. His almost black hair contrasted with his dad's salt and pepper. Albert had a ruddy complexion with deep furrows crossing and converging all over his face. He had thick gray-brown eyebrows and piercing blue eyes like Jack's. The elder Lawson spotted his son and made his way through the crowd. He shook Jack's hand, saying, "Happy birthday, Son." He turned to Carla and took her hand in both of his. "So happy you could join us this evening, Miss Frederick. I'm especially glad to see you survived yesterday's hunt, and you're up and about today. Now, we can all see how beautiful you really are. Love the shirt, by the way."

"Thank you, Mr. Lawson. I know I wasn't pleasant to look at when Jack hauled me in last night. Please, call me Carla." She smiled. "And let me also thank you again for your wonderful hospitality."

"The pleasure is all ours. Please stay as long as you wish," he said, glancing from Carla to Jack and back to Carla.

"Hey, this is quite a party, Dad," Jack observed. "I had no idea you guys had something like this planned! I expected dinner and a cake or something. What's the deal?"

"Aw, we haven't had a decent party here in years. I decided it was about time we had ourselves a big one. You kids have a blast. Excuse me. I have an important call to take in the study." Albert turned and departed the pool deck for the house.

Big O stepped forward. He was a robust, jovial man, balding, but with a full dark beard and forearms like hams. "Come over here and take a look," he said, motioning toward a huge iron drum with smoke streaming from it. Jack and Carla walked over and Big O lifted half the drum, exposing an entire hog roasting over wood coals. "He's been roasting since early this morning and ought to be about right now."

"Is that the one from last night?" Carla asked with a bit of trepidation.

"No. We caught this one last week. It was about a hundred fifty pounds. Just a little biddy thing." Big O grinned. "He'll make good barbeque tonight."

"Thanks, Big O. This is great! Are Buck and the guys here, too?" Jack asked.

"Yeah, they're around here somewhere," he said, glancing around. "Dagny's looking for you two."

Jack took Carla's hand and eased through the crowd, speaking, greeting, and introducing Carla. Dagny dashed forward and hugged Jack. He lifted her off the pool deck in a loving embrace. "Did you guys have a nice afternoon?" Dagny asked, laughing. "We thought you would never leave. It was a nice little suggestion, huh, Jack?"

"It was a great suggestion, Dag. I owe you," he replied.

"Did you finish your story, Carla?" Dagny asked.

"Uh, actually I did. I sure did. But only the first installment," Carla answered, cutting her eyes at Jack. "And it needs major editing."

"Well, you have an awesome subject. Jack is the best of the best when it comes to catching hogs ... and girls, too," Dagny said impishly, then turned and danced away, ponytail swinging.

"Jack, she's so adorable."

"Yes, she is," Jack replied with pride.

"I'll bet the boys are pretty careful with her, knowing her big brother is watching."

"They better be." He smiled, patting his side where, on a hunt, Old Betsy would rest.

Sunama rang a cowbell, said a brief prayer, and invited everyone to eat. There were ample tables around the pool. Jack and Carla joined other couples and enjoyed the delicious food while the band played country tunes. An hour later, Sunama appeared with cake and candles and the crowd sang "Happy Birthday." Jack blew out the candles. Dagny walked over, took his hand, and led him to the dance floor.

The band played a soft Elvis song, and Carla watched as Jack danced with his little sister. Carla entertained the thought of having the same opportunity. She didn't have to wait long.

CHAPTER SIX

As the party died, Carla slipped back to her room and worked on rearranging travel plans. At about ten-thirty, she heard what she thought was a piano. She eased from her room in pajamas and robe, stood at the top of the stairs to listen. A beautiful, yet haunting, melody one might hear in the great room of a New England Inn, or at the Ritz Carlton, Laguna Niguel, her favorite resort hotel on the California coast floated up to her heart. She closed her eyes and allowed the music to transport her to the Ritz's veranda on the bluff overlooking the Pacific. She framed in her mind's eye a lavender sunset kissing a purple ocean, waves crashing against the beach below and bright lights up and down the coast. Creeping downstairs to the dim light of the music room, she was surprised to find Jack sitting at a grand piano. Jack stopped and stood up when she entered the room, but she insisted he keep playing. She snuggled on the sofa and listened, amazed, as Jack finessed the keys in a moving presentation. Fresh on her mind was his gentle caress when they had danced by the pool, a caress she found difficult to reconcile with the man she had observed hunting hogs the day before. And now he caressed her again from the inside out, in a surprising way—simple, yet profound.

Jack raised his eyes to Carla, allowing the last few notes to linger. She stared at him in disbelief, then said,

"That was beyond beautiful, Jack. Where on earth did you learn to play like that?"

"Plato said, 'Music gives a soul to the universe, wings to the mind, flight to the imagination, and life to everything.' Mother taught me." He smiled. But the smile faded in a flash.

"Tell me about her, Jack."

Jack studied the chandelier as if the lights helped him focus his thoughts, or as if he saw her there. "She's beautiful, with long, dark hair like Dagny's. In fact, Dagny reminds me of her. Everyone loved Mom. She loved people, too. She had a wonderful attitude ... always full of life. She was the daughter of a Houston businessman who was headquartered in Paris when she was born. She grew up speaking French and English. Her parents discovered early she was musically gifted and sent her to the finest schools in Paris. In her teens, she was making a name for herself as a concert pianist. Dad was in Paris on a business trip. He was crossing the street, and Mom was walking next to him. He tried asking her for directions in French. Mom laughed at him and began to answer in perfect English. One thing led to another. He courted her for months. Attended her concerts. He brought her here to Brynhild to meet Pop and Grammy. One year after they met, they were married in the chapel. A year after that, I was born. I guess I inherited her love and gift for music. Almost from birth, for many years, she taught me. I still work at it. It's my way of connecting with her, I guess."

"And how did she ..." Carla didn't want to complete the question, but Jack understood.

"Actually, we really don't know how she died. We can only speculate. I've had a hard time even accepting that she's not alive."

Carla frowned in confusion.

"Dagny was a few months old when Mom decided to make an impromptu trip to New York as a birthday surprise for her brother, who was an investment banker there. His office was high up in the World Trade Center's North Tower. It was September 11, 2001. We never heard from either of them again and assumed the worst. She loved Uncle Jack so much she had named me after him. Dad was fine with it. He was, after all, a *fourth*, and said the Lawsons would survive without a *fifth*. Besides, they expected to have many children. But problems developed. I know little of all that. I just know that Dagny was a big surprise. A huge blessing, too, given the turn of events on 9/11. She reminds me more of Mom each day as she matures." Jack's eyes misted, as did Carla's.

"Jack, I am so sorry. I shouldn't have gone there."

"It's okay. It seems like yesterday she was right here sitting alongside me on this bench," he said, stroking it. "Pop was struggling with age when we moved here to Brynhild. Running a spread like this is a huge responsibility. Dad left his job, and he, Mom, and I came here to help take care of Pop and Grammy and run the preserve. I've loved it here from the beginning. But it was Mom who made it a magical place for me."

"Your Grandmother, is she still alive?"

"No."

"So, have you ever played the piano professionally?"

Jack's eyes glazed over. "No. After 9/11, I knew Dad needed me here, and I needed him too. Dagny needed us. Then there was the aftermath ... New York had changed ... the country changed ... a new political whirlwind ... the world was ugly and going mad. You might say the music stopped for me, as for a lot of people. I didn't play the piano for a long time."

"Jack, I'm glad you found music again. Play some more. Please."

Jack obliged, lifting his hands slowly and engaging the keys softly in another astonishing presentation.

She wandered over to the piano and stood beside

Jack, watching the hands that killed with brutality give life and passion to keys. Her heart thumped as every note embraced her.

When Jack completed the piece, the room acquired a penetrating stillness, a hush that wounded yet soothed. Carla studied him carefully. Jack's mind was somewhere far away. Carla wondered where. She also contemplated how juvenile her submission to Arlan was in light of the breadth and depth of the real Jack Lawson story, a narrative into which, it seemed, she was being drawn.

Albert Lawson's baritone voice tenderly broke the silence. He had been standing in the foyer. "That was nice, Son. I can think of only one other person in the whole world who played it like that. Goodnight, *mes enfants.*"

"Goodnight, Dad." Jack turned to Carla. "Any luck changing your flight?"

"Yes. I was able to move my departure to Monday."

Jack smiled. "That's great. Would you like to attend church with us in the morning then catch some lunch?"

"I would love to."

Jack stood and took her hands in his. "Isn't it odd how two total strangers from utterly incompatible worlds have become such good friends in little over thirty hours?"

"It sure is," Carla said, "especially since, at first, I couldn't stand you."

"And now?"

"Umm, you're almost tolerable."

"I'm glad to hear that. Dad makes breakfast on Sunday. Is seven-thirty too early for you?"

"It's never too early for breakfast when someone else is cooking."

Jack nodded. "That's the way I feel, too. Then I guess it's goodnight. Sweet dreams."

"Sweet dreams, Jack."

He watched her climb the stairs and disappear down the hall. He stood in the silence of the foyer for a moment, entertained and dismissed a thought, turned off the lights, and went to his room.

CHAPTER SEVEN

When Carla told Jack she would join them for breakfast at seven-thirty, she had failed to take the time zone into consideration. Carla's smart phone rang at seven o'clock. She knocked it off the bedside table in a blind lunge to silence the alarm then rolled from bed, landing on her hands and knees. She snatched the phone from the floor, killed the alarm, and fell back into bed. Twenty-five minutes later, a dog barked below her window. She opened her eyes wide and sprang straight up, checking the time and panicking. The aroma of strong coffee wafted up from downstairs, reminding her she had made a commitment. Ripping the covers back, she slapped her cheeks, shook herself and leaped from the bed. She pulled her hair back in a ponytail, splashed cold water in her face, brushed her teeth like a child late for school, then slipped into jeans and her Alabama sweatshirt.

Albert greeted her with a bear hug. "Jack tells me you're going to stay another night. That's wonderful."

"Thank you, sir. You're so gracious to allow me." She took a seat at the island and studied the wide-plank pine flooring.

"That's the same wood used at the mill. My dad reclaimed material from other structures torn down a century ago and stored the wood for this house. It was harvested from Alabama old-growth pines. Same is true of that brick," he said, pointing at the waist-high brick fireplace that consumed a whole wall of the kitchen. Logs crackled in the flames. Albert turned back to the stove, saying, "Jack should be down soon. Finished his run. He does a couple of miles every morning to the covered bridge and back, sometimes a little farther, depending on his mood. How's your story coming? Did you get what you came for?"

Carla grimaced. "The story? Umm, I guess Jack didn't tell you."

"Tell me what?"

"Well, Mr. Lawson ..."

"Please, call me Albert. All my friends call me Albert," he said, smiling back at her. "How do you like your eggs?"

"Soft scrambled, please."

"Coming right up."

"About the story. I tried to stop it."

"Stop it? Why?" Albert asked, as he flipped bacon.

"Because I'm afraid I did a gross hatchet job on Jack. The story's not flattering at all. I dashed it off Saturday morning after experiencing my first hog hunt and having a horrible nightmare about it. It's written for consumption by our über liberal readers in Los Angeles and drips with horrid pejoratives about the South, Southern men, and hunting. It makes Jack look like a deranged, degenerate psycho. But, of course, my editor loved it and insisted on going to press. He said it will sell papers. I'm afraid the *World News* is becoming another tabloid. He told me the story will create a firestorm among our readers, and that it should win me an award—an award for yellow journalism I'll deserve. That's why, Albert. I've dishonored your kind hospitality and done Jack a huge disservice. I should be fed to the hogs."

Albert laughed. "An award? That's awesome. How do you like your coffee?" His eyes twinkled.

"Black, please. Didn't you hear what I just said? The story is a travesty. It's going to ridicule your family and your community. As we speak, the papers are hitting the streets with horrible pictures like Jack stabbing a hog with Old Betsy, a gruesome photograph depicting graphic violence. Readers will view it as extreme cruelty. That photo alone will provoke the sensibilities of thousands of animal rights activists who may go ballistic. There's no telling what this may mean for Lawson Preserve, Lawson's Bluff, or Alabama. The media is vicious. If they don't like your politics, religion, or attitude toward them, they can and will destroy you. And writing this story has made me realize I'm one of them."

He smiled at her. "Man, that sounds like a story I want to read! Will you autograph a copy for me?"

Carla wilted. "Aren't you the least bit concerned or angry?"

Albert handed Carla a plate of hot food. "Jack and I have three exceptions to angry."

"What are they?"

"Blondes, brunettes, and redheads."

But she didn't laugh. She wondered whether the Lawsons were gracious, dense, super naïve, or all three.

Albert paused from his work and patted her hand, speaking like a father. "Don't you worry about a thing, sweet girl. We have thick skins in this part of the country. We're used to being stereotyped, lied about, and caricatured by the Left. It's the price we pay for living in God's country. Nobody here reads foreign papers anyway. How's the bacon?"

Carla huffed in frustration and stared at Albert. She wondered what he would think when he read her story, if he ever did. She crammed one whole piece of bacon in her mouth and chewed like a German Shepherd. "It's great. Great. The bacon is great," she said in defeat, shaking her head.

"Help yourself. One thing we have plenty of in Lawson's Bluff is bacon!"

"Did someone mention bacon?" Jack asked, strolling into the kitchen. He had dressed in jeans and a T-shirt. He took a seat beside Carla and nudged her arm with his elbow. "How'd you sleep last night, Carla?"

"Very well, thank you. And you?"

"I always sleep well," Jack said, and then qualified his answer in a serious tone. "Almost always." Albert served Jack a plate then served himself. He stood on the other side of the island, caught Jack's eye and nodded. Jack bowed his head and prayed. "Thank you, Lord, for this day, for this food and for our honored guest, Carla. Amen." Jack's sudden blessing caught Carla off guard. She bowed her head as Jack said, "Amen."

"Carla tells me she's about to make you infamous, Jack." Albert laughed.

"You know, Dad, if this story has legs, if it's as graphic and evocative as Carla says—and who am I to doubt her ability—we may be inundated with new clients wanting to hunt here. We may be able to raise our rates. We could invest more money in the preserve." Jack turned to Carla. "Did you mention the size and ferocity of our hogs and the quality of our hounds?"

Carla shook her head in bewilderment then nodded like a recovering stroke victim. "Oh yeah—size, color, razor-sharp tusks, foaming snout, bloody ears, speed and agility of the dogs. It's descriptive. And the pictures are grotesque. But, let me reiterate, our readers aren't big fans of people who kill animals. They're tree huggers, not hog hunters."

"How do you know? Have you ever done a survey?" Jack asked.

"Well, no. But, Jack, we're talking about California, not Alabama."

"There's hog hunting in California, too, you know."

"There is?"

"Yep. But it's more restricted, more regulated. If guys out there want the total experience, the real deal, they'll want to come to Lawson Preserve and try our more primitive methods. They might even get a shot at Satan—well, I'll tell you about him later. Did you mention in your story about our accommodations and guides?"

"Not exactly."

Jack smiled like a mischievous child. "It doesn't matter. When they call, we'll give them the details. If we're lucky, the story will go viral and put Lawson's Bluff on the map. Try the grits. They're milled local."

Carla managed a smile. "Okay. I hope you guys find as amusing the thousands of radicals who'll freak out over the story. They can be violent. Remember? Portland. Seattle. Kenosha. Minneapolis. New York."

"But this is Alabama," Jack said, quaffing coffee. "We're crazy killers."

"You've been warned," she replied.

"We're not as dumb as we look," Jack quipped, winking at his dad.

Carla rolled her eyes and tasted the grits. "Gosh. Delicious! They would like these in LA."

"She likes grits!" Jack shouted.

Albert chimed in, "My kind of girl."

Carla giggled. "You guys crack me up."

Albert finished his meal and placed dishes away. Carla swiveled her stool toward Jack. "I've been meaning to ask. Where did you attended college—Alabama?"

"I didn't attend college."

"No? Because you ... I mean, you seem so well educated."

"Mom and Dad homeschooled me. I conquered college-level math and English by fourteen. As I mentioned last night, after 9/11, I dropped plans to pursue music, so I had no reason to go to college."

Albert closed the dishwasher, leaving dishes on the counter, and marched out of the kitchen.

Jack paused, giving his father time to get beyond hearing. He lowered his head. "It's difficult for him. He worshipped the ground she walked on. Everything he lived for ... snatched away," Jack said.

Carla nodded, understanding.

Jack admired her face. It was lovely without the muck and vomit. But even with the muck and vomit, she had not been unattractive. Her lips were delicate and well-shaped, turning up at the corners. He adored the trace of dimples in her cheeks and the way her eyes seemed to dance when she talked. But more than her unpretentious attractiveness, Jack was drawn to her straightforward manner—abrasive at times. But she was easy to talk with. And she seemed kind enough, ignorant of the world outside LA, but kind. And she had heart.

"Where was I? Uh, I attended Lawson's Bluff High School my last four years. The Lawson's Bluff Cur Dogs— an odd name for a football team. Cur dogs typically don't fight. They're chase dogs, not catch dogs. I agreed to play ball in the eleventh grade. But I kept hurting guys in games and practice. Parents complained to the coaches. So, I quit. I needed to be able to kill."

"Jack ..."

"After graduation, I wanted to join the Marines and go to war. But Dad needed my help. Coping with life plagued him. If it hadn't been for Big O, Suzanna, and other friends closing ranks around us, I don't know where we would be today. Dagny was a little girl and needed a family. It was hard for us, despite the trappings of affluence and reputation for toughness. My education didn't stop after high school. I continued to read and study. I love learning. But the preserve's my life. Happiness. What makes me me. What keeps me sane. How about you? USC?"

"Princeton. Journalism. Top ten percent of my class. My whole life, I've searched for a story worth telling the whole world. I don't understand why. Isn't it funny what makes us who we are?" Carla sighed.

"Yes, it is."

"I was tapped early by the *World News*. I'm twenty-five. My career is flourishing. But print media is struggling. I have to jump when they say jump or face the ax like others."

Jack checked his watch. "I'll finish cleaning up."

"I'll help you," Carla offered.

Afterward, they dressed for church and joined Albert and Dagny for the drive to the chapel. The weather was vintage Alabama: sunny blue sky, but cool for September.

"Sit with me in the back," Dagny insisted.

Carla obliged. "So, Dagny, tell me what's going on in your world." Carla, Albert, and Jack listened as Dagny babbled about her friends, cheerleading, and the season's first football game ... all the way to town.

They parked and climbed the steps to the chapel. Carla paused at the top and looked back at the town's deserted main street. "Lawson's Bluff in morning brightness, bereft of traffic, so, so pleasant," she said.

Jack nodded and smiled. "It sure is." *And we want to keep it that way.*

They filed through the old doors into the warm and inviting interior. Jack introduced Carla as "a friend of the family, a journalist visiting Alabama for the first time" without mentioning she was writing about him.

"I love these people, Jack. They're so gracious and friendly. But, most of all, genuine and humble," she whispered. "How many members are there?"

"Oh, less than a hundred, I imagine."

Carla made mental notes of the people—proud young parents with a newborn, a child leading an elderly woman by the hand, a young US marine and his girlfriend.

They took seats on the pew Jack had pointed out during their visit the day before. Carla expected to feel awkward and out of place. Instead, she felt at peace. Happy. She whispered to Jack, "This is so special."

Jack smiled, and squeezed her hand. "Destiny," he whispered.

"Huh?" she replied. But Jack remained silent.

Albert sat on the end, Dagny snug beside him, holding his arm. The space to Carla's left remained vacant. She imagined Jack's ancestors sitting there. And she observed the tops of the wooden pews in front of her were polished smooth by a century or more of Lawson hands.

A lean man with silver hair and a strong, calm voice, the preacher had eulogized dozens of Lawson funerals. The deceased were buried behind the chapel. His wife played the piano, and the old man led the congregation in singing hymns. Jack and Carla shared a hymnal. Then the preacher delivered a concise, piercing message without notes or microphone. "Jesus died for you. He is the way and the truth and the life. No one has eternal life except through him. Trust in him," he concluded.

The preacher's words stimulated Carla's memory. She recalled hearing the gospel in a rural Virginia church with cousins on her father's side. But her faith and interest in religion had faded in California while living with her agnostic mother. Whatever faith remained had all but dissipated in the secular, if not anti-Christian, atmosphere of Princeton University.

A spark of revival stirred in her heart. *Is this what I've been missing? Real hope and change?* She thought of the man beside her and wished the old man would look straight into Jack's eyes and say *"You can kill another thousand hogs, Son, but it won't bring your mama back. Only Jesus can do that for you!"* She drifted off into her own thoughts.

The preacher stopped cold in mid-sentence. He stared at the Lawsons as if searching for a secret he knew one of them possessed but didn't know which one. He explored Albert's eyes ... Dagny's ... Jack's. The silence shattered Carla's dreaming. His eyes met hers and lingered. The seconds crashed upon her like Pacific waves. The congregation leaned forward, gripped with expectation, wondering what he would do next. He spoke with great solemnity. "It's been many a year since this congregation witnessed a miracle like the one the Lord just showed me. I can't say what or when, but a significant miracle has already occurred and will impact this body. And all of you will be witnesses. Keep ye watchful." People gasped. He called on a man to close the service with prayer, then sank into a chair as if drained of strength. And he wept.

After the prayer, the people looked up to see the old man still there weeping. Marveling, they eased from the chapel, whispering. A few members, like Albert, approached the preacher in an effort to console him. But he waved them off with a smile. "It's okay. They're happy tears."

They left the chapel and strolled up Main Street to Lawson Mill for lunch. The Hog Rock Café had original brick walls—some with old peeling plaster—pine floors, a fourteen-foot ceiling, exposed beams, and an open barbeque pit where customers could watch the cooking. The walls were adorned with antique gas station signs and pictures of local football teams, cheerleaders, and Old Amos, the high school's cur-dog mascot for whom Jack had named his dog. They took seats at a table overlooking the majestic Chubalatchee River. In its bend, through the trees, they could see their stately home, Brynhild.

"What do you reckon Dr. Allen was talking about in church, Daddy?" Dagny asked.

"I don't know. What do you think?"

"Gosh, a miracle! What could it be?"

Albert replied in a faraway tone that matched the look in his eyes. "I guess only time will tell."

"Did anyone notice how he stared at me?" Carla asked.

"That was truly strange. What was he thinking?" Jack asked, shaking his head.

"I guess you'll have to keep coming back to find out, Carla," Dagny said. Albert smiled and winked at his daughter.

"And why the tears?" Jack asked.

"He said they were happy tears," Albert replied. "Happy tears are good."

LOS ANGELES

Arlan Anderson lounged in his sleek condo, wearing a silk robe and dainty slippers. He perused the morning edition of the *World News*. The front page depicted a strange and hideous beast. He rubbed his hands together with excitement. *This image will compel them to read the story and discover what they're looking at.* That's why the text didn't start until below the fold—so buyers would purchase the paper. He also knew the photograph had been magnified and edited, making the boar look massive and horrible. Its dreadful head was prominent and cavernous mouth propped wide open by a piece of wood. Its tusks and razor-sharp teeth had been Photoshopped to glisten. Eyes, small and dark, contrasted with an enormous snout. A hunter lurked behind the leviathan's grotesque and shredded ears. The photograph captured the man in an awkward stare, as if deranged. Compared to the beast, the men and dogs appeared minuscule, exacerbating the menacing nature of the image and creating a freakish and provocative scene. The editor knew that in a world where people were easily misled, the image of the beast would seduce multitudes, provoking curiosity, hysteria, and action.

His fingers trembled as he turned the page. He gawked at other images—a man drawing a knife from a scabbard, vicious dogs surrounding and snarling at a helpless beast. Across the page, framed in half a dozen color pictures: a gleaming blade, men holding the hog, the knife drawing closer, knife positioned, knife plunging in, blood flowing. Arlan's smile morphed into a grimace. The graphic photographs stimulated his prurient mind. Carla had captured the essence of the brutal sport of hog hunting with unbridled dexterity. "Beautiful," he muttered under his breath. "Beautiful. Sensational. A firestorm." He turned the page and viewed other photos—a dog airborne, dogs dangling from a hog's ear, a bloody hound. "Wonderfully hellish," he whispered. "This will sell papers."

CHAPTER EIGHT

Jack and Carla lounged in Adirondack chairs on Brynhild's broad, manicured lawn and gazed upon the sun-splashed verdant hills. An eagle soared against deep blue sky over the Chubalatchee River. Downstream white-water gurgled over rocks. I could stay here forever, Carla thought. A crow landed nearby and squawked. Carla laughed. "What's with him?"

"He's hungry and irritated, because we don't have food for him to steal. He shows up when we come out here to picnic."

"Jack, is church always so exciting? I mean, what happened today? Unusual or the norm?"

"I haven't witnessed a service like it that I can remember. Do you attend church in California?"

"No, not at all. I'm not really into religion. But I did attend church years ago while visiting my dad in Virginia. So, I was not a total duck out of water today. It was cool. I enjoyed being there. The people treated me so nicely. I needed to hear the gospel again. The message moved me. All in all, a pleasant experience. And, Jack, it was special being there with you, Dagny, and your dad. I'm upset with myself for how I misjudged you guys. I wish I hadn't submitted that wretched story. I would write it differently now." She sighed. "But it's too late."

"Forget it," Jack replied. "I had my own preconceived notions about you. Besides, your portrait of me isn't so far-fetched. What you experienced on Friday is very much a part of who I am."

Carla shifted in her chair, devoting full attention to him. "Jack, is there a subliminal reason you kill hogs? Is it really all about revenge or anger?"

"I promised I wouldn't discuss hogs or politics if you extended your stay. Remember?" he said, meeting her serious eyes with his. Carla nodded. Then Jack smiled and added, "maybe someday we can analyze that, but not now, if that's okay."

"Sure."

As the afternoon faded into early evening, they ambled along the river, skipped rocks on the water and surveyed the changing shadows on the hills. "So, where do you go from here?" Jack asked.

"Flying to Virginia to visit Dad. Then back to La La Land."

"LA's a long way away. I would sure like to see you again. What are my chances?"

"They're pretty good. I would like that, too. Have you ever been to California?"

Jack threw a rock and counted skips on the surface. "Three skips! That's hard to do." He handed her a flat smooth rock. "Here. You try."

"Okay. Here goes ..." She drew back and threw the stone as hard as she could, but it disappeared below the surface. "Hmm, what's his problem?"

Jack laughed. "Yeah, bad rock. No. I've never had a good reason to visit California."

"Well, now you do. I could meet you at Laguna Niguel. The Ritz there is fabulous. I think you'd find the West Coast amazing. Huge waves. Surfers. Beautiful scenery. We could rent a convertible and cruise the coast. Won't you come, Jack?"

Albert stood at the window of his study and watched them. He couldn't help but reminisce, remembering himself and his Mary Catherine walking the same path. *It's about time the boy finds something else to live for.*

They strolled back to the house for dinner. Afterward, Albert and Carla enjoyed coffee while Jack played the piano for them, concluding a perfect day.

Dagny burst in. "A friend called. The news is doing a story on Lawson's Bluff. It's terrible. It's all about Jack and hogs. They make Jack look like a deranged killer! They're quoting the *Los Angeles World News*. Is it based on your story, Carla?"

Carla was speechless. Color drained from her face.

"How could you?" Dagny cried, dashing away.

"I'll talk with her," Jack said, following after Dagny.

Albert shuffled over to an armoire, opened its doors and punched the remote. He searched news channels but couldn't find the report. He forced a smile at Carla. "I guess they'll show it again, or maybe not."

Carla's shoulders sank and despair filled her heart. "I was afraid this would happen. I wish I had never come here."

"Now don't say that. We're delighted you came. This will all be ancient history by morning. Sensational stories like this are a dime a dozen. Don't worry. It's not a big deal." The house phone rang. "Excuse me. I'm going to grab this call." Then his cell phone started ringing. Soon, all the phones in the house were ringing. It was nine o'clock.

Jack and Dagny returned. Dagny took a seat by Carla on the sofa. "I'm sorry, Carla. That was rude. Forgive me."

Carla's eyes misted. "It's okay. Of course, I forgive you. You're justified in being angry. I tried to stop the story when I realized I'd been rash. But it was too late. Journalism can be a rotten business at times."

Dagny smiled and gave Carla a hug. "Jack told me. To be honest, the report is pretty accurate. I've seen pictures like those before. But I've never seen my brother on TV, and when they called Jack a criminal, I got scared. I don't like the way they talked about him."

Carla looked up at Jack. "Jack, I'm so sorry."

"Stop it! I'm not." Jack said with a grin. "I'm going to monetize this. We need to make some T-shirts that say *I killed a hog at Lawson Preserve*. This may bring us hunters from all over."

Carla shook her head and laughed. "You Lawsons are something else!"

Albert walked back in and took a seat in one of the leather chairs facing the sofa. "Jack, Chuck wants us in his office tomorrow morning."

"About what?"

"He's gotten a few wacky calls tonight as a result of this story. Wants to talk a little strategy. Get a handle on things. That's all."

"Who's Chuck?" Carla asked.

"The mayor."

"Oh, great. What kind of wacky calls has he gotten?" Carla asked.

"Just some nuts who ..."

"Saw the story?" Carla asked.

"Yes." Albert smiled. "It's no big deal. Son, play something soothing for us like you did last night. Then I'm going to bed. I'm tired."

PARIS

Warm weather was unusual, so the City of Lights bustled with evening holiday shoppers. A couple sat on a bench in front of a shop and kissed with passion, oblivious to the amused shoppers strolling by.

Rugged Mossad agent Chaim Cohen sat close by them adjacent a street lamp, monitoring the motion of people in and out of restaurants, bars and shops. His chair faced the shops, not the street. On the narrow street behind him sat a driver and car. He faced a door across from him flanked by shops. And stairs beyond the door led to a second floor flat.

Cohen used a newspaper to obscure his face, and down the sidewalk to his left, another agent pretended to window-shop.

"Here he comes," came a voice over Cohen's ear piece.

A man in jeans, sweatshirt, and ballcap appeared from around the corner carrying a bag of groceries. He walked toward them through other shoppers.

The agent pretending to window-shop turned and followed him.

The man stopped in front of the door and glanced about. Just as he unlocked and opened the door, the girl on the bench slapped her boyfriend. Then she stood, stomped her foot and shouted unpleasantries at the young man while onlookers gathered and laughed.

Even before the girl began her tirade, Cohen had walked over to the door and opened his newspaper wide, concealing the man and doorway. The other agent stuck a gun in the man's back and shoved him inside. Cohen closed the door behind them, turned and observed people strolling along the sidewalk as usual. They had noticed the lovers' quarrel but little else. Cohen stepped inside, too.

Sixty seconds later, the other agent escorted a woman down the stairs. Chaim stepped outside and reconnoitered the street. All clear. He opened the door. The agent and woman hastened to the waiting car, got in, and the driver sped off.

Chaim locked the door and strolled away.

CHAPTER NINE

Chaim Cohen stood staring at the puzzling work of art before him titled Rise! Awaken! He studied its depressing black border and inset whiteness punctuated with symbols—the obvious Israeli flag, a tower, the red splotch, what appeared to be an encroaching prehistoric animal scratched into its whiteness from its blackness, the childlike smears of paint. A voice from behind disturbed his concentration, commenting, "the symbols depict the struggle between death and rebirth. The black frame is symbolic of an obituary notice, flanked by a nesting black crow."

Chaim turned and nodded at National Art Curator and former Israeli agent Ariel Akiba. "Thanks for clarifying that. I rather thought it was symbolic of the struggle between the artist and the canvas. A crow, you say? It looks more like a bull ... or a feral hog, perhaps?"

Ariel took Chaim's comment as suggestive. "How interesting and mysterious. The media now rages against young Lawson and feral hog hunting," the rotund Ariel said, gesticulating with chubby hands. "It's tragic how the media complex remains under the control of the global Dark State. This media blitzkrieg is their way of letting us know how upset they are at our recent accomplishment.

But, no, the artist, Gershuni, means it to be a crow—death—not a feral hog. Ah, but look again at the vitality, the life emerging from the darkness. See the flowing blue river of the Israeli flag, the tower communicating renaissance, blood on the flag, the fire-rose—all signs of life, of prophecies fulfilled. How are you, my friend?" Ariel asked.

"Good ... and you?"

"Blessed. It has been a good year." The two men faced the art, standing close together, speaking in hushed tones.

"What better place to discuss mysteries than the cultural heart of Israel, the Tel Aviv Museum of Art?" Chaim asked.

"Most appropriate," Ariel agreed. "And to find you here viewing this particular work is like a sign. Tell me good news of life emerging from darkness, Chaim."

"We have located and now have *L'argent Cle*—Key Money—in our possession. Our special operators have accomplished their mission at long last. Soon, we shall learn whether or not our efforts have been in vain," Chaim replied.

"The museum and the prime minister appreciate your diligence. Please convey our thanks to your people. Once Key Money is debriefed, I'll be eager to do my part," Ariel said.

"Yes," Chaim concurred. "Twenty years is a long time to work a case without the satisfaction of a resolution. Let's hope we have not been played for fools."

"Ah, you think Albert Lawson is that astute? You think he could fool the Prime Minister with such aplomb and benefit from so much intrigue? Personally, I don't think so. And, yet, he does hail from a place called *Lawson's Bluff*—an interesting metaphor."

"We shall know soon enough. Meanwhile, we have dispatched contractors to Alabama to watch over the Lawson family—just a precaution—until we have a complete resolution of the matter," Chaim said.

"Good. Shalom, my friend," Ariel whispered.

CHAPTER TEN

Regret weighed on her shoulders as she looked around Brynhild's grounds. Morning sun splashed against Brynhild Mansion and dew glistened upon the grass and plants. She took a deep breath. Jack placed her things in the trunk of her rental car and lowered the lid. He opened her door and they faced each other.

Jack placed his hand on Carla's arm. "Wish you could stay a little longer."

"Haven't I done enough damage?"

Jack smiled. "There's always room for improvement."

"I wish we could start over."

"Why don't we?"

"I'm not sure the world will let us, Jack. I'm afraid."

"Afraid? Afraid of what?"

"Of time ... and distance ... and forces we can't control."

Jack lowered his hand from her arm. "Forces?"

"Maybe."

"Forces come and go but life goes on," he said, hugging her. She stared into his bright blue eyes for a moment, then she removed her scarf and handed it to him. Then she got in the car and drove away.

Jack remained there holding her scarf, watching her disappear from view. He raised the scarf to his nose and breathed in its scent. Albert emerged from the house and walked down to where Jack stood.

"I like her," Albert said.

"She's upset about the ruckus her story's causing. Her editor refused to stop it. Jerk. Going to be interesting to see what happens now. Life is crazy, isn't it, Dad? I like her, too."

Albert sighed. "Yep. Let's go. The mayor's waiting."

A stout, red-faced man, late forties, with a no-nonsense manner about him, Charles Beeland's tenure as mayor of a once-sleepy town spanned twenty years. He had witnessed its transformation into something fresh and exciting, as evidenced by the dozens of commemorative pictures hanging against the orange pine walls of his office.

"Y'all come in," he called out as Jack and Albert approached his door. The men shook hands and sat down. "You know, I loathe the idea that outsiders may threaten the peace and security of Lawson's Bluff. But I fear we may face turmoil over this ridiculous story about hog hunting and Jack." Multiple phones rang down the hall as Beeland spoke. He leaned forward and perused notes on his desk. "Let's see. We've gotten calls from the Humane Society of the United States, the People for the Elevation of Animals, better known as PEA." He laughed. "And, believe it or not, some holdover in the United States Justice Department called but wasn't clear about anything. I guess he's another bureaucrat sending a message, you know, to inform us their drones are watching. So, nothing new there. The governor's office called, too. And we've had at least one call from a state legislator who's up in arms about hog-dog hunting. I guess the cute little reporter hit a nerve or two out there among the political wild kingdom."

"Any specific threats?" Albert asked.

"Yeah. The PEA folks say they're going to organize a protest and occupy Lawson's Bluff until hunting hogs—with or without dogs—is stopped in Alabama. That's my main concern. Imagine the drain a bunch of lunatics could be on our resources. They might interrupt our unique economy here with the Christmas season only weeks away."

Beeland's secretary rushed in and activated a small TV on a credenza behind the mayor's desk. A young bald woman dressed in black spandex and wearing fishing lures for earrings wagged her finger at the camera and screamed obscenities. Frequent beeps edited her words and obscured her message. But it was obvious. Behind her, protestors wore pig masks and pink tights. They gyrated and shook pictures of small pink pigs and held signs that read: "Save us from Jack the Ripper" and "Pigs are People Too!"

The men watched with amusement until the commentator ended the report and introduced new topics. Then they looked at each other and exploded with laughter. But their mirth soon morphed into sobriety. "You know, I'd say this is a dream," the mayor said. "Unfortunately, this is the world we live in now. It's sad. But we can no longer take this sort of thing with a grain of salt. I'm calling an emergency meeting of my staff, the city attorney, and some of the business community. I think we need to get ahead of this ASAP and be prepared for whatever. Chances are, nothing will happen. But we need to be ready and not get caught in a social, political, and paralyzing storm." He turned to his secretary. "Sara, get the word out. Tonight. Chapel. Seven o'clock. Can you guys be there?"

"Absolutely," Albert replied.

Citizens flooded into Lawson's Bluff like ants streaming to honey. Pickup trucks jammed streets around Chapel

Hill, some holding as many as six men. Hundreds bounded from the pickups and trudged up the hill, packing knives, spitting tobacco, and carrying guns. Hunters restrained dogs. The canines bayed with excitement and sniffed the air for hogs. Ammo belts crisscrossed the chest of a black-bearded hunter. He held a sign, reading: Pigs Ain't People! Another man, dressed in Confederate gray, carried a long sword. Friends and relatives—everyone was related somehow—greeted each other with enthusiasm, slapping backs, hugging necks. The chapel swarmed with people. They raised windows, allowing outsiders to gawk at the proceedings from the yard. Everyone watched news coverage via iPhones, listened to radios, or followed the story via social media. Camo-clad hog hunters leaned against the walls while men in shirts and ties occupied pews with a scattering of women. The rowdy crowd chattered and laughed while dogs barked and howled outside to everyone's delight.

The mayor waved his arms in the air and the crowd settled down. "It's plain to see you all know why we're here. This so-called news report about hog hunting seems to be going viral, and we're getting nasty calls from around the country. We even got an email from someone in Germany this afternoon saluting our efforts to control feral hogs." The crowd roared with laughter. "So, this story has wings. I'm not sure where all this is going, but I think it wise to consider the possibilities and be ready for whatever course this silliness may take. My big concern at this point is we could see an influx of so-called *community organizers* invading our peaceful town, disrupting city services and making our lives miserable. I'd like to hear from you all because it's your town, your businesses. Now don't everyone speak at the same time."

Jack raised his hand.

"Yes, Jack. Go ahead."

Jack stood and faced the group. "Since I'm responsible for this ..."

His statement generated angry shouts. "It ain't your fault!"

"Thank you, boys. By the way, the journalist who wrote the story that started this fuss had second thoughts and tried to stop it from going to press. But her editor wouldn't stop the story. He wanted to stir up the animal rights crowd and sell newspapers. Anyway, I'd say we need to figure out how to take advantage of this free publicity. Hunters all over the country, if not the world, are hearing about our hunting activities, and it's sure to spark interest in hunting here. That's revenue for our restaurants and lodges, and for you hunting guides. As for prospective protesters, I think we ought to figure out how to keep them out of our town. Maybe we can pass an ordinance or create some incentives for them to stay away."

"Okay. But how?" the mayor asked.

"I've been thinking. There's only one road to and from Lawson's Bluff. We're pretty geographically isolated. They can't land a big jet or get here by boat. So, we know exactly how protestors must arrive. They'll have to come in on buses, in cars, something with wheels, or by foot. My guess is protest organizers will bus in paid professional protestors. I don't know why we can't control their movement and dictate their environment and maybe even profit from their presence. If they come in small numbers, good. But, even if they come by the thousands, we can control them if we plan ahead and the law is on our side. The main thing is we want to keep them out of our business district and from damaging our local economy and property. The focus of this meeting should be to devise a plan to subvert the protest. Then they can act up all they want because we'll control the stage."

The city attorney spoke up. "What you're describing sounds like a free speech zone, Jack. I'm not sure that will pass constitutional muster."

"What about loitering?" Jack asked.

"Well, yeah, we can beef up our loitering ordinance.

But how are you going to arrest thousands of people, if it comes to that, with major news media in here filming every move we make and egging them on to violence?" the lawyer asked.

"How about we create another Lawson's Bluff somewhere out close to the city limits? Then we can intercept incoming protesters, escort them to that Lawson's Bluff, get them settled in and let them do whatever they wish until they get worn out and attrition takes over?"

The room was silent. The mayor looked around at the faces and grinned. "What do y'all think? Want to bluff 'em?"

The crowd exploded in laughter.

"We'll sell 'em all the barbeque they can eat!" Big O yelled. "As soon as they run out of food, they'll think pigs taste real good."

A lean, middle-aged man standing against the wall raised his hand and the mayor recognized him. "Mayor Beeland, I own thirty acres of farmland just inside the city limits 'bout a quarter mile off Lawson Road. It's got an empty trailer, a barn, some old chicken houses, and electricity to it. I'll deed it to the city for fifty thousand dollars and provide owner financing if the city will give me the right to buy it back in the same or better condition, and for the same price."

The crowd erupted in laughter again.

The mayor waved his hands in the air. "Now Bill, that's a reasonable offer. But I'm not sure the council will go along with something so binding on the city, even for your sterling property. Would you consider a month-to-month lease with an option to buy?"

"Okay, I can do that," the man answered with a wink.

"The city council meets tomorrow at seven. I'll ask the city attorney if he would be so kind as to draft a document to that effect." Then the mayor turned to his chief of police. "Chief, I'll need you to get with FEMA. Give me an assessment of tents, emergency trailers and such on hand and available in case visitors don't bring their own. Big O and the rest of you boys, get us up some hogs for our guests. We don't want to be inhospitable. And, Sheriff, we need to be on the lookout for out-of-state tags. We want to make sure our visitors find Lawson's Bluff without a hitch. I'll call the airport angels at Birmingham International and alert them to watch for incoming protestors and keep us informed. Some of you boys who are good with hammers and saws need to get out there to the entrance to Bill's property and make us a nice town sign." The crowd roared approval. "Bill, how's the road into your property?"

"It could use a little scraping. I have a small dozer, and I'll make sure it looks really nice, depending on the lease terms." He chuckled.

Jack whispered to Big O, "Does Bill still have Ben?"

"Last I heard, he did," Big O replied.

The mayor continued. "Let's monitor developments and think about how we can best serve humanity and our community. Y'all be thinking how we can make Bill's property look like a town. Hopefully, this will all just go away. But, in case it doesn't, let's be prepared. I urge all of you to keep the details of tonight's meeting to yourselves and you may wish to attend the council meeting tomorrow night. Agreed?"

"Agreed," they shouted.

The preacher raised his long, bony hand.

"Yes, Doctor Allen?"

The old man arose and faced the crowd. "Let's not forget. This might present an opportunity to minister to some lost souls."

The mayor waved. "So, you'll understand what we're up against, listen to this." He punched his phone, playing a message.

I'm with the People for the Elevation of Animals. We are closing ranks with other organizations for a united front against the mistreatment and murder of hogs in Alabama. You are evil savages. You will be hearing from us. Murderers!

Outside, a clever citizen hooked up a speaker to his iPhone and commenced broadcasting live news. Men and dogs alike howled in unison at reports about the "murder" of innocent feral hogs in Alabama. People used their phones to share graphic photographs and loitered on Main Street. "Let's go murder some pigs," a man yelled.

Jack and Albert wandered among the swirling horde, speaking with friends. A hunter asked, "Jack, have you heard the latest?"

"What now?" Jack replied without emotion.

"The United Nations has issued a statement against animal cruelty in the United States, accusing Americans of 'violating international norms and standards of humanity.' And the president of Russia hunted down and shot a 500-pound Russian boar, landing front-page in European newspapers. He was shirtless, kneeling beside his kill."

Jack laughed. "Five hundred pounds? That's a big hog. Sounds fake."

Another chimed in. "Yeah, he's extending an invitation to you to hunt in Siberia. *The New York Times* is alleging you're in collusion with Russia!"

"This is insane," Jack replied. "This media delusion is making Jack Lawson a catchword for animal cruelty. And now I'm a Russian spy?"

The local newspaper editorialized about the controversy, writing, "This is a ridiculous, senseless, hysterical, media frenzy. Killing feral hogs is one's civic duty!"

Business owners and concerned citizens packed the city's small meeting room, shouting demands for immediate action to save their livelihoods. Mayor Beeland presided over the chaos. "Calm down please. Just calm down," he said, waving his hands in the air like he had the night before. The people hushed. A heavy man in overalls poked his hand up.

"Yes, sir. Please speak," Beeland said.

The man jabbed the air with his index finger as if poking an invisible chest. "All I got to say is this. What them radicals did to other US cities ain't happenin' here!" The crowd broke into applause. Beeland waved his hands again and the people stopped clapping. The man continued poking. "This ain't Portland. We need a plan, 'cause if they try and pull that bull here, somethin' bad's gonna happen. Now, I'm jest tellin' you."

"And that's why we're here," Beeland replied. "We're preparing for an invasion of radical protestors. Ladies and gentlemen, the world outside Lawson's Bluff is suffering from HDS—Hog Derangement Syndrome." The people roared. "So, here's the plan—as was pointed out last night, the only road to Lawson's Bluff forks east at the city limits. The road to *New Lawson's Bluff* will fork again, providing a simple traffic detour. I want a flurry of activity to explode on the outskirts of town. Let's get busy creating a new town to receive our dubious guests. Who's with me?" The crowd roared approval. "Okay. We've divided the work into projects and listed equipment requirements. Sign up and show up for Operation New Lawson's Bluff. Remember, we must not let these radicals invade our lovely town!"

Next morning, as the dew evaporated in Alabama sunshine, truckloads of cheerful men converged at the entrance to Bill Farmer's property. They laughed and chanted, "Pigs are people, too." A camo-clad man climbed on a tractor that featured a drill attachment and excavated post holes, while others readied the posts. The men erected a grand sign in minutes. *Welcome to Scenic Lawson's Bluff.* Then another: *GPS UPDATE. TURN HERE.* They covered the chicken-wire sign with civic club logos. Others hurried down the gravel road in pickups to the abandoned chicken farm and placed a *Town Hall* sign on Farmer's trailer. They erected a flagpole and installed a Coke machine by the trailer door. Dozens of men surrounded the barn and sprayed it white. Men strapped themselves with rope and scurried up ladders, placing a cross atop the barn. They planted a makeshift historic marker in front conveying the barn's unique story as the *First Darn Barn Church of Alabama*. At the preacher's request, the local sawmill donated enough lumber to build bleachers and a large stage inside the barn. Busy workers high-fived each other as they raced about their work, banging nails home, zipping boards with screaming Skilsaws, drilling holes for electrical poles, and running wire.

Ladies arrived at noon, lugging baskets stuffed with homemade delights and sweet tea for workers. A plump woman rang a cow bell, shouting, "Come and get it!" Hungry workers sprawled on the grass or perched on tailgates, relaxed, feasted, and laughed together, celebrating the rapid growth of the new town and discussing new ideas, like a park. After lunch, throngs of joyful townsfolk descended upon the chicken houses with boxes of tools and loads of building materials. They attacked the empty sheds like expert contractors—ripping, smashing, banging, slinging paint brushes, pouring concrete, hanging plywood, and shaping the decrepit structures into a top-notch flea-market mall. A convoy of trucks arrived with FEMA trailers in tow. Men lined them up on "Main Street."

Main Street led to an attractive twenty-acre pond fed by a stream through dark woods on its opposite bank. Those woods rose hundreds of feet on either side of the stream and curled around the pond to form the greater perimeter of the new town. The pond's presence effected a scenic tranquility reminiscent of the Carolinas or New England. During daylight hours, its surface shimmered, reflecting trees and blue sky.

But nightfall transformed the stream, woods and pond into a menacing land of assorted wild critters like big cats and ravenous feral hogs. And in the pond, lurked Bill Farmer's unique feral hog extermination service, a twelve-foot alligator called Ben. The gator floated below the shimmering surface and scrutinized the sudden activity with interest.

In the evenings, Hog Rock Café delivered barbeque plates to the site. Men set firepits ablaze. Local musicians entertained and the people partied. Square dancing broke out. And fireworks set the night sky alive with color. As word spread of the revelry, more people came, and the once-deserted acres attained a carnival-like atmosphere.

The makeshift town took on an appearance of habitability as competitions broke out among merchants to heighten its credibility. They built facades in front of the trailers and leased space in which to sell their goods and services to the potential influx of buyers. They hung flower boxes and set out barrels of mums to decorate their respective stretches of Main Street. Men delivered generators and strung lights across porticos, giving the town a warm and inviting ambience. Enterprising young men sold cold drinks to visitors who streamed in from the countryside to witness the strange but exciting activity of a town appearing out of nowhere. By the weekend, New Lawson's Bluff had taken on the appearance of an odd but unique and charming village. People patted each other on the back, excited and eager to receive guests and extend Southern hospitality.

CHAPTER ELEVEN

Virginia

Carla cringed as she watched the evening news. "Again, we wish to warn our viewers of the graphic nature of the photographs we're about to show." The statement was intended to attract viewers, not warn them away. The screen filled with bloody images of dogs and men—and Jack stabbing a hog. She thought of Jack and the good people of Lawson's Bluff. *They should hate me for casting them in this light.* She was astonished that her story was receiving global media attention. Paranoia gripped her. *Are mysterious and powerful forces responsible for Jack's media lynching?*

A popular and attractive commentator narrated. "Years ago, our former president, by the stroke of a pen, used his executive powers to elevate and take control of climate change policies. His goal was to streamline sustainability initiatives and skirt legislative oversight. Enforce a new federal agenda. Grant himself sweeping power over a myriad of issues that, up until then, were the exclusive province of the states. That was then. This is now. This evening at the White House, the new president tweeted, 'I love barbeque. May have to visit Alabama soon!' He rescinded all those previous executive orders. But don't we still have an obligation to protect critical sectors of our ecosystem, and prepare the United States for the significant impacts of animal migrations and population changes? Because these migrations can't be avoided. The changing climate will not allow it," she said.

Carla's dad entered the den. "How about a glass of wine?" he asked with a calm typical of a man who had taught American history for thirty years. Carla had inherited his hazel eyes and blond hair. But Richard Frederick's hair was now gray. A man of average height and build, he was ambivalent about fancy homes, clothes, cars, and furnishings, unlike his ex-wife, whose self-esteem was fed by things and shaped by appearances. When Carla wanted an injection of the world, she visited her mother—but when faced with life questions and issues of the heart, she sought her father. Richard handed Carla a glass of wine and dropped beside her on the sofa in his khakis, wrinkled blue cotton shirt, and loafers. "More news about your story?"

"As a matter of fact, yes," she answered with exasperation. "Dad, I can't believe this trivial feature story is being exploited like this—all this attention focusing on Jack Lawson and the killing of feral hogs in Alabama. I mean, I knew it might have an impact on radicals in California. But this global hysteria is disconcerting. No, disturbing. Listen to this! The United Nations has issued a resolution condemning the slaughter of wild hogs. Give me a break. Feral hogs are a huge nuisance. Even I get that. They devour everything in sight. Do billions a year in crop damage. The sows possess an atomic procreation rate. If they're not exterminated, the darn things will overrun the planet in six months! The UN is nuts. This hog thing is blown way out of proportion. And to think I started it all. But, you know, I'm beginning to think I've been used somehow. What I submitted to the *World News* was tabloid at best. But it's being hyped around the world. Why?"

Richard peered over his glasses at her. "News is hardly news anymore, Carly. It's now about advancing an agenda. It's a sign of our times. You, of all people, should know that."

"But whose agenda and why? What's the end game? Have I been so cloistered in the media world that I've become unable to distinguish truth from falsehood or even care to make the effort? After all, look what I did to Jack Lawson without stopping to think about the consequences. We in the media say nice things about people we know, or like and agree with. Then discredit those we don't know or don't relate to. It's true. We have little regard for truth or objectivity. By not telling the truth, the whole truth and nothing but the truth, we recklessly advance some agenda. Journalism is deceased!"

"Perhaps you've answered your own question."

"Have I? Is it that simple, Dad?"

"Of course it is. Despots have long aspired to advance their schemes through propaganda. History teaches us that. Evil men—Marx, Goebbels—can do great damage when they monopolize the narrative and manipulate or suppress speech. But, in the final analysis, all men are boats at the mercy of the lighthouse. They have two choices: They may trust and obey the lighthouse, or they may indulge their own lies and crash upon the rocks."

"Gosh. You sound like Jack Lawson, Dad."

"How's that?"

"We had a philosophical discussion, of sorts. Jack asked me cryptic questions, like, 'if anyone personally fails to oppose evil, is that person personally advancing evil and abandoning truth?'"

"Martin Luther King said something like that. And you answered?"

"I don't remember how I answered. But I'm beginning to relate. We can't trust and obey the lighthouse without setting our sails in opposition to the rocks." Carla looked into her dad's eyes. "Daddy, I'm disillusioned about this mess I've created. Where do I go from here?"

Richard smiled. He put his arm around her and gave her a squeeze. "You need to ask the lighthouse. Tell me more about the intrepid Jack Lawson."

"Well, he's not the stereotypical Alabama redneck I imagined he would be. Tough as nails. Tall. Built like a boxer. Strong as an oak tree. He's self-educated, intelligent, and well-mannered—when he's not carving up some unfortunate hog. And, oh! Get this. He's a stupendous piano player! His mother died in the 9/11 attack. He was so shaken by her death at the hands of terrorists that he flipped out in his teens. I think his hog hunting—he's been killing hogs for twenty years—is some kind of coping mechanism. He can be intense one moment, then relaxed, gentle, and empathetic the next. But his obsession with this certain hog, the Majority Leader, is scary."

Richard couldn't help but chuckle. "*The Majority Leader?*"

"A massive black and white boar he's been tracking for months. No one else has ever seen it—only Jack. He swears this particular hog is as smart as a human being, maybe smarter. That makes killing the Majority Leader a dangerous challenge for him. And Jack loves a challenge. But I'm afraid one day, Jack will catch up with him. Or, worse, Majority Leader will catch Jack."

"Wow. Why does Jack call this boar the Majority Leader?"

"Jack hates powerful politicians. He thinks many are bought and sold. He's angry the government didn't take stronger measures against terrorists and prevent 9/11. Remember how the 9/11 terrorists learned to fly big planes ... in US flight schools?"

"Yes, I do."

"And he refers to lesser male hogs as cronies and to piglets as minions."

"What does he call sows?"

"Don't ask."

"I must say, he has a sense of humor." Richard laughed.

"That he does. But the pain and hurt I've seen in his eyes is heartbreaking, Dad. I think he could benefit from counseling. I think he has deep wounds that need healing."

"And so do we all."

"There's more. Jack told me the Majority Leader is not even the big fish. He said there's another feral hog out there so large and so cunning it dwarfs the Majority Leader in stature and intelligence. He told me he was alone in the woods one night in a blind, using night-vision equipment. He glimpsed this boar in a close, yet fleeting, encounter. He said it was like witnessing a goliath shadow with glowing red eyes. According to Jack, the creature glided by the blind as if floating on air."

Richard's eyes grew wide. "Yikes. What does he call that one?"

Carla leaned toward her dad, looking him dead in the eyes. "Satan."

Richard studied his daughter for a moment. "You have feelings for this guy?"

She pondered the question before answering. "Two guys. There are two guys in there. One I like. The other frightens me."

CHAPTER TWELVE

Hogs saturated the underbrush. Dogs weaved in and out of the tangle, barking, howling, flushing pigs into the open, stopping some cold. Using rifles, Big O and Turnip dropped three on the spot. Men loaded dead hogs on one truck and gathered the dogs onto another. Old Amos was missing.

Jack checked his GPS. "I'm going after Amos. GPS has him a mile away!" Jack yelled from his truck. "Anyone want to come with me?"

"Yeah, I will," Buck answered. Buck wasn't as tall but, like his best friend, he was solid and tough.

"You sure, Buck? I don't want to get you in trouble with family."

Buck was married with two children. "Yeah. They won't mind. Anyway, this shouldn't take long. But we do need to find you a wife!"

Jack grinned. "Yeah? Why's that?"

"So I can get some rest."

Both men loved Amos, a shepherd pup they had named for their high school mascot. Buck's competent brown eyes flashed. "Why does Amos always have to do his own thing?"

"He's a maverick. That's for sure." Jack smiled and accelerated. "He's stationary. Must have a hog bayed!"

"Then we need to get there fast," Buck said.

They stopped within a hundred yards of Amos's position. "GPS says he's at the center of this clear cut. See the thick underbrush there?" Buck asked, pointing.

They bounded from the truck, stood still and listened, but heard nothing. The motionless terrain troubled them. "Maybe he lost his monitor," Buck suggested.

Jack shook his head. "Not likely. Let's be careful." Buck chambered a round in his Glock .45 Model 21. They strapped lights on their heads and moved obliquely toward the GPS mark indicated on the screen—treading a spiral until within several feet of the signal. They eased forward, Buck at point, nervous finger on the trigger.

"I see Amos, Jack. He looks dead to me."

Jack burst forward and stooped down to Amos's carcass. "Look at this, Buck. In his teeth. Half of a white ear."

Jack removed the ear from Amos's teeth and examined it under his light. He shivered as he stood up and surveyed the cold dark woods. "Amos had the Majority Leader. He had the Majority Leader, Buck. While we were back there shooting a few small cronies, Old Amos was trying to bay the Majority Leader by himself." Jack paused and listened for movement in the woods. "He's being very quiet. But he's still here. I know him. He's probably concealed at the edge of the woods. Watching us. Sizing us up. Learning. Boasting in his heart about killing Amos. He's corrupting the rules again to his advantage. Making our next fight for freedom from his curse more difficult for us to win." Jack drew Old Betsy, waved the blade in the air and bellowed like a man shot through the gut with an arrow. Buck jerked, squeezing off a round. The bullet ricocheted off a rock.

"Buck! Be careful!"

"Jack! Why'd you holler like that? Let's go, man. You're creeping me out," Buck shouted back.

But Jack ignored him and continued to yell. "You'll make a mistake! When you do, I'll be there with Betsy! You hear me? And go tell your master, Satan, that I'm not afraid of him, either!"

Jack slipped Old Betsy back into the scabbard. He scooped the dog's body from the damp earth and trudged back to the truck without another word.

Buck trembled as he followed Jack. With his finger still on the trigger, he watched for movement from stump to stump, taking care to cover their retreat from the ghastly field of death.

The Majority Leader stood his ground like a hunk of cold steel, bereft of emotion. The man's outburst didn't move him. He stood motionless and aloof in thick brush at the tree line—seven feet long, seven hundred pounds of muscle, lethal tusks. He could barely see the men. Nor did he need to see them. Instead, he observed them through his keen senses of hearing, smell, and intuition. He analyzed them, learning from their cautious retreat from the field of battle, and memorizing their scent. He knew one of the men, the one whose scent was on the dog. He didn't know the other. They had passed with their backs to him. He had contemplated charging and killing them both. That's what his less intelligent, less experienced colleagues would have attempted. He could have been upon them before they would have known what was happening. But he suspected, from the familiar sound of metal engaging metal, that one of them was armed. And the Majority Leader preferred, like human predators, to err on the side of caution.

The black-white fiend listened as the truck engine roared. The woods filled with blinding light. Rays flashed through the foliage. He closed his eyes to prevent light from discovering him, and waited. Soon, the noise of the men was less than that of a squirrel eating a nut in a nearby tree. A gentle drizzle fell. The dew of heaven accumulated on his back, formed beads of water and rolled off, soothing him, but also stirring his mind to action as rain always did. Then he bolted from the brush and assumed an easy trot along a familiar trail through the forest. Every creature in his path, great and small, dashed for cover. Before light came again, he would be miles away. *It's too bad they took the flesh with them. I'm always hungry, and especially eager to eat out the substance of those who oppose my agenda.* Against a light wind, into a deep state of darkness, he vanished.

After driving Buck home, Jack stopped by the maintenance building for a shovel. Agonizing over the loss of Old Amos, he drove to the orchard behind Brynhild. He parked close to a pecan tree where he kept a pile of stones. Memories flooded his mind of walks there during the cool of the day. He saw Amos running circles around him, begging him to throw a ball, a stick. Jack's tears united with the rain-soaked ground, making the soil more personal and malleable. It was eleven o'clock, cold and breezy. The wind whipped through the tree branches, whining like injured rabbits. But Jack took little notice of the weather. Love compelled him forward. Labor kept him warm. He shoveled blade after blade of the rich muck and flung it in a pile. When excavation took him waist deep in the pit, Jack climbed out. He placed the hog's ear back in Amos's teeth, wrapped the body in a piece of canvas, and gently lowered his friend to the bottom. While cold rain stung his face, neck and arms, Jack stood beside the grave and wailed. He covered Old Amos in mud and stone, threw the shovel in the truck bed, and drove away.

It was midnight when Albert met his son at the back door. "Hey, Jack, I was getting worried about you. Big O said you and Buck left the hunt at about six o'clock looking for Amos. I tried your cell phone but it went to voicemail. I was finally able to contact Buck. Boy, you're a mess."

Jack sat down on a bench in the mudroom and pulled his boots off. "Sorry, Dad. I turned my phone off. Old Amos is dead. I buried him out in the orchard."

"Buck told me. I'm sorry, Jack. He was a wonderful companion and a valiant hunter. I know this is difficult for you."

"He died trying to hold the Majority Leader. We must have reached him about the time he bought it, because he was still in one piece. A minute sooner, we might have saved him. His heart must have exploded during the fight."

"The Majority Leader, huh? How do you know?"

"Amos took his ear off. The white one. It was still in his teeth."

Albert studied his distraught son with trepidation. He was weary of hearing about the Majority Leader and wondered if the creature of Jack's obsession was not an invention of his imagination. *For sure, a dead Amos is not his imagination.* He didn't wish to aggravate his boy's obvious grief with further questions. "You have some calls on the answering machine in the study," he said.

"Who called?"

"Carla Frederick."

Jack looked up. "She did? What'd she say?"

"She's upset about the TV coverage her story has sparked."

Jack shrugged. "So, what's new? Who else?"

"A knife maker in Double Springs wants to talk with you. He said it's urgent. And a fellow named Macon Jones wants to hunt Lawson Preserve."

CHAPTER THIRTEEN

Puffy white clouds hung against the blue sky like floating bales of cotton. Inactivity marked Lawson's Bluff. Most of the people were at New Lawson's Bluff, transforming an abandoned chicken farm into a miracle village. A crisp Monday morning found them laboring with joy. One man asked, "Ain't it amazing what we can accomplish without government regulations, licenses, fees, and meddling?"

"Indeed," his friend replied. "It's like we've turned back the pages of time and reentered history during frontier days. Back then, pioneers were free to take risks and suffer consequences without all the red tape."

"Exactly! Did you know that hunters have been spending nights out here, fellowshipping with friends, and taking turns throwing chunks of pork to Ben? They love it here."

"Yep. And square dancing in the barn has become the thing, followed by gospel music. We have great local musicians."

"And the evening revival has grown to hundreds!"

Enthusiasm intensified at the arrival of the first outsider. The people welcomed the tall, lanky young man like a celebrity. He had bushy brown hair and a matching beard.

"Welcome to Lawson's Bluff. We're so happy you're here. Where you from, son?"

"Oregon," Johnson Sampsel replied. "I'm painting my way across the country. I've never seen the southeastern US, tasted grits, or met a southern belle. I was driving east on I-70, near Topeka, listening to the radio, and kept hearing about Lawson's Bluff and dogs and hogs. All the talk intrigued me. I decided to find this place and capture the drama on canvas."

"Well, honey, you look like you've been here all your life in them boots, ragged jeans, and that corduroy shirt," a lady said.

Men pumped his hand, and the ladies hugged and pampered him, asking, "Where are the others?"

"I'm not sure," he replied, looking about. "Are you expecting others?"

"Oh, yes. Many more," the ladies gushed.

"I must get busy, then," Sampsel replied. He set up his easel with haste, and began to paint his surroundings. Not far away, the boys were roasting a pig. Sampsel filled his canvas with the colorful image of men roasting a hog over an open pit. A local art enthusiast acquired the painting on the spot for two hundred dollars cash. Sampsel jammed the money in his pocket and grabbed another canvas. He grinned and looked around for his next theme.

The ladies brought him sweet tea and barbeque, and bragged on his work as if he was the incarnation of a Dutch master. By the end of his first day, the young man had five-hundred dollars in his pocket for three small works. People were bidding against each other for his next painting.

An attractive young lady strolled up to Sampsel as he put away brushes. "How's it going so far, stranger?"

"Awesome. I haven't spent a penny on food, drink, or rent. Nor am I paying a forty percent gallery commission. I love Alabama!"

"Would you like to go to the barn with me tonight?" she asked.

"Should I bring a canvas and some paint?"

She smiled the way girls do when they know something others don't. "Whatever rocks your boat."

Mayor Beeland's phone rang. "Mayor, we have news that a bus crammed with prospective occupiers has been spotted heading toward Lawson's Bluff."

Beeland rolled his eyes. "Here we go. Okay. Alert the sheriff's office. Dispatch deputies to intercept the bus inside the county and escort it."

Jubilation broke out and the people scrambled to prepare for the contingent of protesters. The deputies waited along the route in the parking lot of an abandoned Dairy Queen. As soon as the bus passed, they raced ahead of it and waved for the driver to follow them.

The bewildered driver dared not disobey. He followed the deputy's blazing lights down the old road. The Lawson's Bluff High School Cur Dog Marching Band greeted the occupiers. People lined the road waving pink flags and shouting, "Pigs are people, too." As the puzzled driver and passengers approached Main Street, the band played Auld Lang Syne. The occupiers gawked from the bus windows. Some smiled and waved. Others appeared agitated or frightened. The rotund deputy stopped and confidently stepped from his car and strolled back to the bus. The driver, who had a troubled history with the law, opened the door with great dread.

The deputy grinned. "Welcome to Lawson's Bluff."

The driver flashed a weak smile, twitched and stuttered. "Tha-thank you, officer. But Lawson's Bluff ain't on our schedule."

The deputy tilted his head and frowned. "Aren't your passengers here to occupy Lawson's Bluff?"

"No, sir. These are tourists from the Daisy Days Retirement Village. We're just passing through. We do have a stop in Montgomery though."

The band played on while the mayor stood by with a key to the city. The deputy stepped up into the bus and stared at the old men and women. They stared back with ambivalence. He patted the driver on the back. "Your driving is exemplary, sir. Just follow me. I'll get you back on the road to Montgomery. Thank you for your cooperation, ladies and gentlemen. I hope you enjoy the rest of your trip." The octogenarians applauded. The bus turned around and away they went.

"We need to work on the traffic pattern," the mayor noted, watching them go.

Soon after the sojourners had departed, another bus arrived. The driver turned right off the main road, saw the town sign, and approached New Lawson's Bluff. A major news network truck and camera crew followed. The people reassembled and resumed their places. The drum major turned to the band and awaited his cue. People waved pink flags and shouted, "Pigs are people, too." The bus stopped. Mayor Beeland nodded at the drum major, and the band started up. While the camera crew raced to catch unfolding events, occupiers sat on the bus, allowing reporters time to set up and film the action.

Everyone recognized the first radical off the bus, bald-headed Kirsten Radner, profane leader of the People for the Elevation of Animals. She strutted around in black tights like a bantam rooster, glaring at the smiling faces. Fishing lures hanging from her ears slapped against her face and neck as she jerked one direction then another, flabbergasted at the reception. Others with her were dressed in pink tights and pig masks. They disembarked behind Radner, waving signs. Young people, including college students, stepped from the bus. And behind them emerged rough looking men with criminal eyes. Radner launched a volley of obscenities, demanding, "Who the hades is in charge here?"

A single black ear in the woods beyond the pond stood straight up. The band ceased playing. Mayor Beeland stepped forward with a large key and presented it to Radner. "On behalf of the people of Lawson's Bluff, it's my pleasure to welcome y'all. I hereby present y'all with this key to our city." The mayor grinned and handed Radner the large key.

Radner's eyes morphed into embers. She spit in Mayor Beeland's face, cocked her arm, and sent the key sailing toward the pond. An alert cur dog dashed after the key, retrieved it, and dropped it at her feet. The crowd erupted in laughter. Radner responded by shouting inventive profanities. She insulted the mayor, good citizens and town. Then she shouted, "Where's Jack the Ripper?" The women in pink tights waved pictures of little pigs and chanted, "Pigs are people, too! Pigs are people, too!" The townspeople joined in. When Radner at last paused from her profanities, the people applauded. She screamed as if they were gouging out her eyes. She ran back aboard the bus and stared wide-eyed through a window, as if staring into her own asylum.

The camera crew wasted little time setting up a satellite feed and swinging into action. But with Radner sulking on the bus, there was little action to report. Lured by the smell of roast pork carried on the breeze from the other end of Main Street, the reporters strolled off to acquire some for themselves.

Radner's tawdry company of protestors stirred about without purpose, gathering their backpacks and awaiting instructions. People of Lawson's Bluff mingled with and engaged them in conversation. "Did you have a pleasant trip? Where are you from?"

As the sun dipped below the horizon, a disgusted Mayor Beeland got in his truck and departed. The band disbursed, and the horde of greeters eased away, too, except those waiting to attend the evening revival service. Gospel music filled the barn.

The bus driver demanded Radner get off the bus so he could leave. She cursed him but complied. And he roared away.

The old preacher drove up, dressed in overalls. He tipped his fedora hat at the pink ladies and invited them to joined the service. But they declined, squirming in his presence. He entered the barn where hundreds had gathered. They closed the giant doors, and he began to preach on "the days of Noah." The soft light from inside the barn glowed through cracks. One young occupier strolled over, peeped through a crack and listened.

Outside the barn, protestors set up tents and hunkered down for the long haul. They were, after all, being paid well—by whom, they didn't know. Radner and the women in pink tights stripped to the waist and danced in a circle around a firepit, mocking the revival service, and chanting to Mother Gaia, mother of the earth. The rough men with criminal eyes walked among the tents, looking for vulnerable young women. The Colorado college flunkies smoked dope around a campfire. And, from the other side of the lake, twenty feral hogs observed these strange events and patiently awaited their curtain call.

Deep darkness fell outside the First Darn Barn Church. The world devolved into a screaming, wicked stupor, as if a cloud of evil had descended and enshrouded the once-happy makeshift village. The revival continued until well after midnight, when the barn doors were flung wide and the people streamed forth with lanterns aglow. They walked silently to their cars as though traversing a graveyard. A slight drizzle began to fall as the last tail lights disappeared from view.

Across the lake, the dew of heaven rolled off the Majority Leader's grimy back. The hog stood motionless for two hours, calculating and listening for sounds of life, but heard none. The humans were gone, stoned or dead asleep. So, in the remaining darkness of a nascent morning, he eased around the pond with a dozen cronies following at a distance. Behind them were innumerable sows, gilt pigs, and a few piglets—his own sounder of pigs. They approached the chicken houses, rooting in the damp earth, making their way toward the aroma of roasting flesh the men had abandoned among the coals.

The smell of humans was everywhere. But that was to be expected. They had observed them from across the pond and then watched them go. A snorting noise coming from the strange, flimsy structures the humans had left behind startled the sounder of swine. They bolted in an instant and scattered toward the pond. But the Majority Leader was unconcerned, curious about the sound, thinking it, perhaps, derived from something edible like an injured animal. The sounder relaxed and resumed feeding. Less intelligent, less experienced young boars waded into the pond's shallow water, had a drink and sparred with one another. A few young females approached the water's edge to watch them.

On occasion, the Majority Leader's curiosity competed with his intelligence. The occupiers had erected their tents in the "park" adjacent Main Street and the giant hog strutted among them, enthralled by the snorting noise and wanting knowledge of it. He had heard this sound before when passing near the encampments of humans. The noise had never harmed him, and he was now fearless of it. In fact, he adored it. He eased alongside a tent and listened to the melodious sound from within. His hooves sank deep into the wet chestnut muck as he stood spellbound for a long while. The snorting sound had a soothing effect on the sore ear the dog had taken off a few days before. Noting the Majority Leader's calm demeanor, several sows and their piglets entered the area and rooted around tents. They were quickly joined by a few smaller boars in the two-hundred-pound range.

The Majority Leader watched in amazement as a small piglet scooted through an opening in one of the strange structures and emerged from it unscathed. He approached the thing with caution, sliced open the tent with his tusk and sniffed its contents. The strong smell of human flesh filled his nostrils, exciting him. Not since his youth along the Rio Grande had he tasted humans. He pushed further through the flap and noted an object protruding from a peculiar ground covering. It was a strange entity. Indeed, he had never seen anything quite like it. There was a heavy, delightful odor emanating from the thing that invited a taste-test. There were five nut-shaped buds atop it to choose from. He lowered his snout and severed the large one and the one next to it and devoured them. A stream of warm crimson flowed from the flesh, and a larger thing jerked beneath the cover. As the Majority Leader was about to take a second bite, the balance of his bald-headed-snack, Radner, sat straight up and screamed like the sirens that sounded in bad weather.

Ben, without causing a ripple in the starlit water, had eased to within a foot of a small gilt wading in the shallow water. Ben dug all four claws into the lake's clay bottom and lunged forward, ensnaring his unwary prey within powerful jaws. She squealed at the top of her lungs. Ben thrashed her in the water, backing up, twisting, pulling her below. The commotion shattered the night. Except for a few eyes glued shut by alcohol or drug-induced stupors, every eye opened in New Lawson's Bluff. Occupiers appeared from tents and, like awaking into a bad dream, found themselves surrounded by the very feral hogs they had come to save.

Majority Leader hated the demonic creature's ear-splitting screech. He bolted, entangling himself in cord and tent fabric. He lowered his head and charged into the night, hawing and trying in vain to disengage from the alien material adhering to him. The faster he ran, the tighter the thin substance seemed to cling. He sprinted toward the security of the woods, making himself a pledge to be extra cautious in the future and stay hidden from humankind.

Pandemonium ensued. Young boars scattered in all directions. But the sows launched a vicious, full-scale attack on the emerging humans they perceived as threats to their young. In blind rage, the sows ripped apart tents and flesh and everything they encountered in a reign of terror. Two criminal-eyed men darted through the chaos, attempting to reach the barn. But two observant sows spotted them and gave chase, catching them halfway to the door. The sows employed razor-sharp tusks to slice the men's calves and Achilles' heels. Prostrate on the ground, the men howled and flailed to no avail as the sows sliced and diced, leaving them limp and shredded. Another large sow charged a fleeing human wearing pink tights, penetrating the space between the runner's legs. The woman collapsed upon the animal and, by reflex, grabbed its pointy ears. She held tight like a catch dog, and disappeared into the darkness screaming for Mother Gaia to save her. Pigs and people, too, raced in circles, slashing and being slashed. Six college students sprinted toward the entrance to New Lawson's Bluff and the highway beyond, neglecting to look back. Screams and sobbing filled the air. While sows inflicted havoc, mindless piglets swarmed in and out of what was left of tents. Like rioters in an American city that had defunded the police, they looted food and other provisions with impunity. Amidst the grunts, screams, and clacking of teeth, a calm voice from a cell phone speaker could be heard. "This is 911. Do you have an emergency? Pigs are what? I'm sorry, I can't understand you. Say again. What's that screaming I hear? People are what? What is your location? Hello? Hello?"

Daybreak found the press slinking into the open. The commotion they had slept through from the safety of their sturdy RV had subsided to soft moans. They stood in abject silence and stared across the park toward the barn. Occupiers limped about like living dead. Bloody bodies were strewn from Main Street to the barn. The cameraman took a sip of steaming black coffee. "What in the world happened here?" he asked the reporter beside him.

"Beats me. Looks like a fight broke out."

The cameraman winced. "From the look of things, it was a knife fight."

"Were we not told these people were non-violent?" the reporter asked.

The cameraman shook his head. "You can't trust the media."

Sirens screamed. A convoy of emergency vehicles raced toward them. A medic dismounted from a rescue truck and jogged over. "What happened here?"

"Knife fight," the cameraman replied.

The medic nodded and dashed away.

The cameraman turned to the reporter. "Shall we crank up the cameras?"

"Nah. No story here."

And area hospitals overflowed with wounded occupiers who were heard asking doctors and nurses, "How fast can you get me out of Alabama?"

CHAPTER FOURTEEN

Jack leaned against the Rover and scanned the western horizon. October blue sky reflected against the lenses of his military-style tactical sunglasses. He checked his phone. Four o'clock—the hunter's estimated time of arrival. Jack heard the engine's whine and glimpsed a bright speck in the distance. He reached inside the Rover and activated the headlights and flashers. The pilot executed a wing wave, landed on the grass runway and taxied to the hanger. As the pilot stepped from the craft and retrieved his gear, Jack sauntered over to the twin-engine Beechcraft and greeted him. "Mr. Jones, Jack Lawson." The young man stood about six feet, and tipped the scales at one-eighty. He wore an olive bomber jacket over a black T-shirt, jeans, and hiking shoes.

"Call me Make," the man replied. "My friends do." They shook hands, placed his gear in the Rover, and got in. Macon Jones removed his sunglasses and pushed his red hair back. He looked over at Jack and grinned. "So, I have a question for you."

"What's that?"

"Are pigs people, too?"

Jack smiled. "You better believe it. Been watching the news, huh?"

"Yeah. You've stirred up a hornet's nest." Jones laughed.

"There's a pig or two frequenting the preserve that may be people in disguise. Or maybe they're hybrid beings. I don't know. But if you want to hunt super smart hogs, you've come to the right place. Have you ever hunted feral hogs before, Make?"

"Not the way you do. You're a far more honest hunter than I am."

"Well, without dogs, you're lucky to ever see a hog," Jack explained. "You might from a blind where they're being fed. Even then, as I'm sure you know, they're clever, elusive creatures."

"You ever lose dogs?" Make asked.

Jack studied Jones' freckled face for a moment. Jones returned his stare. "Unfortunately, yes. It's risky business for dogs and hunters alike. Just lost two last month. One died at the vet after a brutal fight. The other caught a boar all by himself. Old Amos—I raised him from a puppy. The boar killed him. He had taken on one of the biggest, meanest, and smartest boars around—a hog I've been hunting for a while now. I've about resolved I can't take this one with dogs and a knife. I need to lure him to within a thousand meters and shoot him with a fifty-caliber."

Jones shifted in his seat. "How do you know the hog that killed your dog is the same hog you've been tracking?"

"Because this particular hog had one black ear and one white ear. And now he has just one black ear. The other—the white one—was in my dog's teeth."

Jones nodded. "Sorry about your dog." A short silence followed as Jack exited the paved road and turned onto dirt.

"The cabin is rustic, but comfortable. I've got some steaks in the cooler. We'll chill tonight. Get out early," Jack said. "Okay with you?"

"Sounds great." Make smiled. "So, Jack, do you have any interests beyond hunting?"

"Piano."

"No joke? Never would have guessed it," Jones said, gesturing with his hands. "The man whose hands catch vicious hogs goes home after the hunt and plays his piano. They failed to mention that on the news. So, are you as good on the keys as you are with a knife?"

"I'm okay."

"I love piano music. Do you know any Rachmaninov?"

"Yeah, sure. It's some of my favorite music." Jack smiled.

"That's outstanding—a Renaissance man."

"So, what's your background, Make?"

"Military. Investments. Subcontracting," Jones replied. He looked out the window. "I used to take piano lessons as a kid in junior high school. I'd leave school and walk to this lady's house for a lesson twice a week. One day, I stopped by the school's office to check out for my lesson and both the football coach and the principal were in there. They made fun of me. So, I dropped lessons that same day. Never went back. I've always regretted letting them get to me. Couldn't stand anybody thinking of me as a sissy. Anybody ever make fun of you about being a piano player?"

Jack turned left down yet another dirt road. "Yeah, every now and then," he replied. "Some guys came here to dog-hunt boars a few years ago. Somehow it came up I played the piano. So, this big, loud guy started taunting me about it. They'd been drinking. He got in my face." Jack paused.

"So, what happened?"

"Betsy and I walked away. I didn't want to spend the rest of my life in a penitentiary."

"Who's Betsy?"

Jack patted his knife. "He made me so angry that had I not left when I did, I might have taken him out. Of course, he thought I was a coward. The next morning, the dogs bayed a giant hog. I got there first, tossed the hog and straddled it. A couple of my guys got the dogs off. Getting mad dogs off a mad hog is about as dangerous as dealing with the hog. The dogs are insane and vicious at this point. They'll attack you, too, and rip your face off. So, I'm about to stab the hog and this guy comes barreling in and shoves me off, thinking he's going to make the kill. When he caused me to let go the boar's front leg, I rolled to my feet and kept going. I knew what was about to happen. The hog reared up, turned on this guy and nearly killed him. It was a brawl to end all brawls. He was screaming like a baby. We let the dogs go. Everyone freaked. For a minute, it was a bloody free-for-all. Fortunately, the hog took off with the dogs in pursuit but he never stopped again. It took us forever to get the dogs back. We had to air-evac that guy to Birmingham." Jack laughed and cut his eyes at Jones.

"What a story!" Make shouted.

The men cooked the steaks, enjoyed them in front of the fire and talked strategy for the morning hunt, then took bunks at ten o'clock. Four hours later, they eased away in the Rover for the preserve's mid-eastern woods. The night was clear and moonless. They traveled a mile. Jack parked off a foot path and they hiked another quarter-mile, using night vision goggles. Except for the hoot of an owl, the woods were dead still and silent. "The weather may be too nice," Jack whispered. "Clouds and a gentle rain would be better." They reached the blind where Jack had put out corn that morning, got inside and waited.

The blind overlooked a vast opening in the woods where hogs were known to move from dense woods toward wetland. "We'll be lucky to see hogs on such a clear night. We'll see," Jack whispered. Macon nodded and scanned the field for game. Coyotes howled in the distance.

Hours passed. Close to daybreak, they spotted a few small does. Otherwise, the night was uneventful. They chatted on the way back to the Rover.

"Tell me more about the Majority Leader. What's his signature?" Make asked.

"The first time I ever saw him was right back there. I had been in the blind for going on twenty-four hours, from dawn until dawn. I'd placed water sources and feed all over the field. Just about every critter you can imagine strolled through. But no hogs. I was surprised. Then, just before first light, someone opened the gate. I was so sleepy that at first, I almost missed the action. A couple dozen small pigs crossed the field from east to west. But they weren't grazing. They were running. As they ran, they scooped up feed and kept running to the west side of the field into the woods. I had never seen anything like this. Then came another dozen, from east to west, same thing— snatching up corn, racing to the woods. I never had a good shot. They were all too small, anyway. At first light, the field was vacant. I needed sleep. So, I decided to break off the hunt. I shouldered my rifle and walked out on the field to see how much feed was left, then followed the path the small pigs had taken. As I paced along the western wood line, observing every tree and noting every thicket, poof! There he was, standing not five yards away, his black and white ears at attention. It was like he was introducing himself. He was huge. The sight of him at such close range stunned me. He had waited there for me. I had become the hunted. My rifle was slung. He could have been on me in an instant! Instead, we stared at each other for about two seconds. He hawed. I recovered my composure and drew my sidearm, thinking he was going to charge. But as soon as I moved, he disappeared through the brush. I eased over to where he had stood. Guess what I found?"

"What?" Make asked.

"Feed. All over the place. The small pigs had been delivering him breakfast in bed. I can't help but think that, somehow, the Majority Leader had conditioned or trained, if you will, his followers—I call them cronies—to do his bidding. He stayed in the shadows while they took all the risks. That's pretty amazing, don't you think?"

"That is amazing! I've never heard anything quite like it—in the animal world, that is," Make agreed.

"So, you asked what his signature is. That's it. I've looked at other blinds, off in the woods, away from the open field. I find feed. That's why hunters rarely see big hogs on our fields. The Majority Leader has taught them. He's scary smart—seems to learn from observation—and is capable of strategizing."

"And he's not the only one."

"How's that?"

"It appears Jack Lawson learns from observation, too." Make smiled. "So, how do we catch this big boy?"

"I don't know. I'm still trying to figure it out. Think like him, maybe? But how does a being who's not so adept at evil think like an evil one? Anyway, that's why I wanted to start you out on this particular blind. Now that you know the story, where would you like to go from here?"

Make smiled. "I have this thermal drone ..."

CHAPTER FIFTEEN

Albert looked up from his work and smiled as Jack entered the study. He leaned back in his chair and put his hands behind his head. "Hi, Son. Thanks for allowing me to interrupt your hunt. How's it going out there with the Jones fellow? You guys having any luck?"

"Not so far. We sat in a blind till dawn. Saw some small deer but that's about it. Jones wants to use a thermal drone to locate hogs and drive them into the open. Should be interesting. We'll see. What's up?"

"I'm going out of the country for a week or so with a friend. He should be here any minute to pick me up."

"Really? Where're you going?" Jack asked with surprise.

"France. Meeting some old friends in Paris. Suzanna's taking Dagny out of school and going on a church retreat with her to North Carolina. You'll have Brynhild all to yourself for a while, with one exception. We'll have some men using the guesthouse while I'm away. They'll be coming and going on business. And maybe entertaining others. So, don't be alarmed if you see people coming and going from the guesthouse. Just take care of Jones. We'll catch up when I get back. Feel free to call me if you need to."

"Yes, sir. Have a good trip. Be careful."

Albert stood up and shook his son's hand. "Thanks. You too, Son."

Driving away from the house, Jack passed a dark Ford. The driver looked familiar, but Jack's thoughts had turned to hunting hogs with a drone. He wondered if the Majority Leader could evade heat-seeking drone technology.

He arrived back at the hunter's cabin, finding Jones dressed in camo and checking his gear. "You're going to love this," Make said. "There's nothing like thermal imagery as seen from the air. If there are hogs or anything else out there, we'll see them long before they see us. We can drive them right into our sights. Show me where we are on the preserve."

Jack nodded and took out a simple map, pointing with a pencil. "Here we are. This is the main house, about two miles northwest of us." Jack wiggled the pencil down the left side of the map. "The river." Then he tapped the map, pointing to and drawing the pencil down the right side. "These woods to the east are where the hogs hang out and rest up. It's a tangled mess over there. Very different terrain. Rock and thickets. But water is scarce. A few small streams there, but they usually run dry as a bone. Hogs can't stand it long without water. So at night, in hot, dry weather, they run for the low muddy areas close to the river. On their way over to the lowland, they check out our fields." Jack pointed below the southern border of the preserve. "Down south is grazing land. We like our hunters to stay well north to avoid shooting cows. What are you thinking?"

"Where's the blind we were in last night?" Make asked.

"Here." Jack pointed. "Between where we are now and the main house."

"Why don't we just go back there tonight and use the drone to monitor activity in a radius around that field? Unless you have a better idea."

"Sure. That's fine with me," Jack said. Macon's phone chimed and he began texting, as if attending to urgent business.

About midnight, the men returned to the blind, took up positions and launched the drone. In a few minutes, the machine was a mile away, imaging anything in its view that radiated heat. Macon watched the screen with great expectation. "Let's see what's out tonight. Watch for white bodies that look like pigs. There! See them?"

The screen filled with white forms that looked like mice moving in the woods below. "Looks like hogs to me. What do you say, Jack?"

"They're pigs. I can tell by the way they're moving. Looks like a couple of sows and a litter. Let's have some fun. See if you can move them our way." Jack watched as Macon worked the controls, maneuvering the craft to the east of the pigs and coming in close to the trees. At once, the white forms on the screen scurried in one direction then another as Macon moved the drone left and right, moving them westward.

"How cool is that?" Jack chuckled.

Make nodded. "Very cool. They're a good mile away, though. Let's keep looking and see what we can find closer to us."

Jack watched as Macon flew the drone in an arc over the preserve. "Recognize that?" Macon asked.

"That's the house."

Macon hovered high above Brynhild for a moment. Jack could see a car parked near the guesthouse, the white figure of a man walking near the car.

"Can that guy hear the drone?" Jack asked.

"Maybe. Do you know who he is?"

"He must be one of our guests staying there this week. But I haven't met any of them yet. Are you recording?"

"I am, indeed," Macon replied.

The white image of another man joined the first and the two figures ran toward the front of the main house. Macon kept the drone's camera focused on the men.

"What's this?" Jack demanded, alarmed. Four additional figures appeared to be landing in a boat from the river. They pulled the boat ashore and made their way toward the house. The first two men from the guest house appeared to assume prone positions on the front lawn. They were armed with rifles. The men from the river advanced at a trot. Two fell and were still, followed by the other two. "These guys must have silencers. Otherwise, we'd be hearing the shots. I've got to get home!" Jacked shouted. "Let's go!"

"Maybe that's not such a good idea, Jack. We don't know who the good guys are and who the bad guys are. If we go rampaging into the midst of this, we may end up like those four dudes on the lawn. Stay calm. Let's think about this for a minute."

Jack reflected for a moment. "Good point. I'll call the sheriff."

"Look. Another vehicle is arriving," Macon said.

They watched as two men stepped from what looked like a cargo van and ran toward the two remaining shooters. All four men loaded the bodies of the four limp ones, carried the bodies to the van, and sped away.

"My battery's getting low. I've got to get the drone back."

"Wait! Let's see what these guys do."

"Sorry, Jack—I can't. We don't want the drone falling out of the sky on top of these guys! I've got to get it back."

Minutes later, Macon landed the drone at his feet. Jack called and described to a deputy what they had seen on the monitor and emphasized that the intruders had appeared well armed.

"I'm calling the sheriff now," the deputy said. "We'll meet you at the house. But make sure you don't get there before we do, understand?"

"Got it," Jack replied.

The quarter mile trek to the Rover consumed precious time. As they tossed gear in the SUV, a plane roared over the treetops.

"Now who could that be?" Macon asked.

Jack floored the accelerator. When they reached the airstrip, he turned toward the hanger, conducting a quick reconnaissance. Macon's plane was still there, but all was quiet. Jack approached the house with caution, slowing to a crawl well short of the entrance gate.

"No signs of police yet," he said.

He pulled off the road and waited. Flashing lights appeared behind them. Jack stepped from the Rover and stood by the door, allowing deputies to recognize him. Sheriff's cars and an Alabama state trooper slowed, then proceeded by him. He drove toward the house, following the last police car. The officer stopped short of the formal driveway, blocking Jack from driving farther. Jack pulled off the road and waited. Twenty minutes elapsed. The deputy stepped from his car and walked back. "All's clear. You can go in now. The sheriff's up by the front of the house."

The sheriff was a tall, thin man, age fifty, with a viselike grip. He had a stern face, dark eyes, thin lips and a brusque manner.

"Sheriff, this is Macon Jones."

The sheriff nodded at Macon. "Mr. Jones. May I see your driver's license?"

Macon handed it over. The sheriff photographed it with his cell phone.

"What have you found, Sheriff?" Jack asked.

"Nothing at all. Your doors and windows are secure. No evidence of tampering. All's quiet here. No signs of a struggle. We're looking for blood but none found so far. Are you guys sure of what you saw?" he asked.

"We can show you the video and you can see for yourself," Jack said.

"You have it with you?"

"Yes, sir," Macon answered.

Macon retrieved the monitor from Jack's SUV and played it back. The sheriff watched with intrigue. "Okay.

I'm convinced something happened here tonight. But what? No blood. No bodies. They were shooting a movie, for all I know. I'll need to sequester that device as evidence and download it. You can pick it up at my office tomorrow. Meanwhile, we'll be on the lookout for suspicious vehicles in the area. That's about all we can do for now. Off the cuff, I'd say drugs are involved somehow," the sheriff said.

"One more thing, Sheriff. We heard a small plane overhead as we were leaving the woods. It was right over the trees. Must have taken off from our field," Jack said.

"Drugs," the sheriff repeated.

"Did you guys find a boat? Any footprints near the water?" Macon asked.

The sheriff shook his head. "They cleaned up after themselves well—a little too well, I think. Professionals. We'll come back and look around again at first light."

"Sheriff, it seems strange to me that drug smugglers would come here to our front yard to transact business, killing people, hauling bodies away, and flying off from our strip!"

"I agree, Jack. But that appears to have been the case. It's a good thing your family was away. This could have been tragic. It's also interesting that Mr. Jones happened to video these events. You may wish to have a lawyer present tomorrow, Mr. Jones, when you come for your equipment. We may have some questions for you," the sheriff said, looking hard at Macon.

"I understand, Sheriff. You'll have my complete cooperation."

The sheriff turned to Jack. "These grounds are now off limits until we have a chance to further investigate in the morning. It's a murder scene now. Jack, I don't want you, or anyone," he said, glancing at Jones, "walking around disturbing any evidence we haven't yet discovered, or making tracks, or removing anything. I'm posting a deputy here tonight. Understood?"

"Yes, sir," Jack replied.

CHAPTER SIXTEEN

On the way back to the cabin, Jack and Macon reflected on the night's events. "No offense, Make, but, you know, like the sheriff said, it is odd we just happened to video these activities tonight."

Macon watched Jack's weathered, shrewd face as he replied. "I agree. But it was a complete coincidence, Jack. I assure you of that. If I had any knowledge of it, why would I have blown my cover by showing you what was happening?"

"Yeah, I've already considered that. Unless ..."

"Unless what?"

"Unless you wanted to ingratiate yourself to me and gain my confidence for some reason," Jack said. "But that would be a bizarre way of going about it," he added, realizing the illogic of his own thought.

"Look, I'm here to hunt hogs, not video murders. If I knew this—whatever it was—event was going down, the last thing I would do is compromise my cover by exposing the actors. Now the sheriff has my name and my video. On the other hand, had I not stumbled onto them, it's highly likely that neither you, the sheriff, nor anyone else would have ever been the wiser. Maybe the sheriff's right—it's a drug deal gone bad. But why they would trespass on a prominent property like yours to transact criminal activity is a good question."

"I know. I can't help wondering who they are. It's totally perplexing and makes me really mad, too." Jack's mind was far from hunting. *What if this guy who calls himself Macon Jones wanted me to see something and believe it? But it was all just staged? But, again, why would something like this be staged for my consumption? And why would he record it?* "So, do you want to head back to the blind or call it a night? Your call."

"Well, since the sheriff has my monitor, I guess we should call it a night."

Macon slept soundly, Jack fitfully. Macon arose early, started a fire and cooked a hardy breakfast. Jack smelled the bacon and joined him. They ate and sipped coffee in front of the fire without much conversation. Jack simmered over the events of a few hours earlier and was keen on visiting the sheriff to see what might be learned.

"Get any sleep?" Macon asked.

"Not really. I'm eager to see what the sheriff has to say this morning. I couldn't stop thinking about it."

The sheriff was in uniform, unlike the night before when he'd been off duty, dressed in jeans and a coat he had grabbed on the run. His demeanor struck Jack as more formal and serious. "Gentlemen," he said, shaking their hands. "Please, sit down." He studied Macon for a moment, observing his trim build, thick neck, and rough hands.

He pushed a box toward Macon. "Your equipment, Mr. Jones."

"Much obliged, Sheriff," Macon replied.

The sheriff turned to Jack. "We went over your place with a fine-toothed comb beginning at first light, Jack. No blood. No bodies. No shell casings. Nothing. We searched the river in both directions for a boat. Nothing there either. The video is all we have to go on and, unfortunately, we managed to erase it in an attempt to copy it to a PC. So, we have zero, zip."

Jack felt his face turning red.

"I know. I know. We made a huge mistake, and I take full responsibility. But what's done is done. We've also had zero sightings confirmed of a van in our area last night. And zero reports of a plane being seen landing or taking off from your property, except the report you gave us. Therefore, with absolutely no evidence that a crime has taken place, this case is closed. I'm sorry."

"That's it? No questions?" Macon asked.

"No questions," the sheriff replied. He stared silently at Jack.

Jack stood up. "The video was real. The plane was real," he said.

"I saw the video, Jack," the sheriff said. "But without it, I have nothing. And even with the video showing little more than infrared images, I have nothing without a body. Case closed. I'm as disappointed as you are."

"Last night, you said you would have some questions for Macon," Jack said, motioning toward Macon who was now standing, too.

"We conducted a background check. You're in good company," the sheriff said. "I suggest you boys go shoot some hogs." His tone was imperative.

Back in the Rover, Jack turned to Macon. "I think it's time we get better acquainted, Make. I want to know everything there is to know about you."

Macon nodded. "Sure," he started without hint of offense. "Born and raised in Lowndes County. Joined the Army after high school. Airborne Ranger. Did time overseas. Got part of a degree. Spent a few years in the investment business. Got bored. Learned to fly. Became a contractor. Several tours overseas doing embassy work. Came back to the states. Started a small business. Made peace with God. Saw you on TV. Decided to go kill hogs."

"Married?"

"My wife died a couple of years ago," Macon said with deep sadness in his voice.

"I'm sorry," Jack replied, glancing at Macon and pausing before asking another family background question. "Do you have any children?"

"Nope."

"What do you mean by embassy work?"

"I worked security at various US embassies as a subcontractor for the government."

"What kind of business did you start?"

"I train security personnel for government and private entities."

Jack paused to think. "What's your company called?"

"Jones Global."

"So, I guess the sheriff discovered this, too," Jack said.

"I would assume so."

"I don't buy it," Jack said.

"You don't buy what?"

"That they accidentally erased the video."

"They didn't," Macon said.

"What do you mean?"

"My equipment is programmed to automatically erase a video in sixty minutes."

"You knew that and didn't tell the sheriff?"

"I couldn't afford for that video to get into the wrong hands. It was better to be safe than sorry. But don't worry. I downloaded it to my phone," Macon said, holding his phone where Jack could see the video playing.

Jack quickly pulled off the road and studied the video.

"It doesn't matter though, Jack, the sheriff said himself that, even with the video, he has no body, no blood, no case. Remember?" Macon asked.

"I remember." Jack smiled, pulling a small, round can from his pocket. He pinched some green stuff between his fingers and stuck it in his jaw, then offered some to Macon. "I feel like hunting."

"No thanks," Macon said, declining the spinach.

"So, I have a little secret of my own," Jack said. "In the heat of all of this, I almost forgot. Then I remembered during the night—one reason I couldn't sleep."

"What's that?"

"I'll show you."

Jack turned into the airfield and steered the Rover past the hanger to a stand of small trees. He stepped from the Rover and walked toward the trees. Macon followed.

"See this?" Jack asked, pointing to a small box on a tree.

Macon shrugged. "A bird feeder?"

Jack lifted its door. "This is a motion-activated camera. As you can plainly see, it's designed to capture activity on our airfield. When activated, the video records and the recording is accessible via an app on my phone." Jack slipped his phone from a pocket and activated the app. In seconds, they were watching yet another video—Macon's plane landing, their first meeting. Then a second video appeared—a larger plane landing. A van entered the picture. Four men jumped out of the van and loaded four heavy bags—body bags—into the waiting craft. The men reentered the van and it departed. The plane turned and took off. "The quality's not great. But it's clear what's happening. I didn't see a tag on the van or numbers on the plane. Did you?" asked Jack.

"Negative," Jones replied, frowning.

"It'll be interesting to see what the sheriff has to say about this," Jack snapped. "Let's go."

"Not so fast, Jack," Macon said, stopping Jack in his tracks.

"Why not?"

"Look, Jack, I know this is none of my business, but think about the sheriff's reaction to my drone video. That was evidence his people didn't destroy. And he knew it. It was almost as if he was relieved there was nothing there. He let us off far too easy, Jack. At least to me, as an outsider looking in, he wanted to close the case. Why?"

"I think he made that pretty clear. No bodies," Jack replied.

"But what if he's deliberately turning a blind eye? What if it was a drug deal and he's in on it? What if he's bought and paid for? What if we present this new video and he impounds your phone and his people accidentally erase it, too? What then?" Macon asked.

Jack studied Macon's face as he pondered his questions. "We've known him for years."

"It's your call, Jack. Like I said, it's none of my business. But if I were you, I'd give it some time and thought before rushing back to the sheriff. This video still doesn't identify the actors. You still can't produce a body. Just saying ..."

"Maybe you're right. I'll sleep on it." Jack sighed. "I'm sorry this has interrupted your trip. I'll discount our fees for the time you've missed in the field."

"Not a problem," Macon replied.

"Mind if we run by the house? I'd like to check on things," Jack said.

"Sure."

Jack's mind swirled with questions as he drove to the house. He noticed a car outside the guesthouse. He parked and walked to it, pausing to study the car's Virginia license plate. He knocked on the door and waited several seconds while Macon stood by the Rover and watched. A young man of average height and build opened the door. He was dressed in slacks and a golf shirt, had short, dark hair and wore black-framed glasses.

"Morning. I'm Jack Lawson. And I assume you're our guest this week?" Jack asked.

"I'm John Phelps," the man replied, extending his hand.

"When did you arrive?"

"Just got here, actually. Nice place. Thanks for allowing me to use it."

"Sure," Jack said. "How was your trip? Looks like you came a long way. Virginia?"

"Yeah. Tidewater area."

"So, what brings you to Lawson's Bluff?"

"I represent an industrial concern that's interested in the area. Just here to look around and take notes, so to speak," he said.

"Enjoy your stay. I'll be hunting most of the week. But if you need anything, here's my number." Jack handed the man a card.

"Okay, thanks, Jack." Phelps smiled, glancing toward the Rover and Jones. Jack turned and departed for the main house. Macon followed.

They entered through the back door. "Would you like some coffee, Make?"

"I'm good, thanks," Macon replied, looking around.

"Make yourself at home while I check messages." Jack headed for the study.

Macon strolled into the foyer and noticed the piano off to his left. He entered the music room, took a seat on the piano bench, and picked at the keys.

Jack sat down at his dad's desk and activated the message recall on the phone. He scanned various papers on the desk. A frantic voice implored Jack to return the call—a fellow from Double Springs, Alabama, who wanted to make replicas of Old Betsy, engraved with Jack's signature. "I can sell these knives to hunters. But we need to strike while the iron is hot, Mr. Lawson," the man said. Jack rummaged through the top desk drawer, looking for a pen or pencil with which to jot down the man's number. He opened the drawer wide and searched among its trivial contents. He saw a small stack of business cards held together by a rubber band. Out of curiosity, Jack slipped the rubber band off and sorted through the cards. As boredom was about to compel him to replace the rubber band, a certain card disturbed him. *Jones Global / Macon Jones 757-757-7575.* The card showed a post office box number in Virginia.

Jack listened to Macon's strained attempt at playing the piano as he stared at the card. He replaced the rubber band around the others, placing them back where he had found them. Fingering Macon's business card, he wondered how it had come to be in his father's desk.

CHAPTER SEVENTEEN

Albert studied the billowing clouds. He considered the years and reflected on the precious times lost, all the Christmases past. She loved Christmas. The big jet taking him to Paris was not unlike the one that had carried them to Alabama to meet his family. She was so young then, and demure for a girl raised in the lights and sounds of Paris. He remembered her there dancing around a fountain, skipping across the expansive lawn beneath the Eiffel Tower, strolling among the shops, and shaded by a colorful umbrella at their favorite sidewalk café.

The young men had gawked at her. Who could blame them? Her disarming smile, inviting blue eyes, chestnut shoulder-length hair, fair skin, all wrapped in the latest fashion as her adoring father had provided. How was it possible he had lost her? Was it because his many business trips left her vulnerable? Why, he wondered, had he not seen it coming? When she was all that mattered in the world, how could he have been so careless, allowing her to go to New York without him? Had he only been there with her! Then he remembered the thousands of families whose lives had been shattered by the events of that fateful day, families whose loved ones would never come back. His sadness turned to anger at the thought of it. At least, Jack had found a way to cope. He, on the other hand, never had.

Albert had avoided all contact with women since her departure. Substitutes were unthinkable. The company of other women offered little repose from the anguish of his error. They reminded him of a failure that pierced his heart like a thorn of transgression. Lost in his thoughts, hours into his trip, Albert closed his weary eyes and dozed.

Chaim Cohen's voice brought him back. "Albert, Albert," he said, nudging him. "You should see this." Chaim pointed at the screen in front of them.

"Where are we?" Albert asked.

"An hour out from Charles De Gaulle," Chaim replied.

Albert pressed one plug of a headset into his ear and watched the monitor. He recognized the scene—proceedings of the United Nations General Assembly in New York, where a wall appearing as a golden shaft of light featured a halo-like symbol that glowed roundabout its leaders. Flanking the golden shaft were two huge screens filled in living color with images of carnage. The slaughter was not an infliction on humans by humans. It was a massacre by humans of wild pigs.

The men watched as a reporter explained. "Behind me are images of a new creature concern being discussed at this imposing body of international representatives, the United Nations. The question being raised here today is whether the inhumanity toward animals, as seen in these offensive images, is not in some way more inhumane than the taking of human life. After all, it is human life that is in so many respects, destroying the planet, while these innocent creatures are struggling to survive in whatever habitat has not yet been taken from them."

Albert leaned forward slightly in his seat. "See that picture? That's Jack, isn't it?"

"Yes," Chaim replied. "I believe it is."

"The United Nations, too? This is absurd. Has the whole world gone mad?" Albert asked.

"You get used to the madness after a while, Albert. In the land of Israel, my people are killed for sport. But the United Nations turns a blind eye. In Israel, it is the people who are labeled pigs. In America, pigs are called people. To understand these UN ministers of mendacity, you must first understand they are agenda-driven. Their madness has meaning and purpose. But you need not worry. You see, this is not directed at Jack. It is, rather, a message for Israel. And as brutal as these images appear, it's not even about flesh and blood, but about who controls the ring. The message is clear—the Dark State is omnipresent, omniscient, and that, while we may have won a skirmish, we will not win the war ... in their opinion."

Albert nodded agreement. "For our struggle is not against flesh and blood but against rulers, against authorities, against powers of darkness and spiritual forces of evil in heavenly places," he said, trying to quote the book of Ephesians.

"Exactly," Chaim said.

They were soon on the ground and departed the plane, then the terminal, in haste, shadowed by a second agent. Chaim escorted Albert to a waiting sedan, and they sped away on a circuitous route to the Israeli Embassy. The driver stopped in front of a tobacco shop along the *Rue Jean Mermoz*. They hurried from the car into the shop. Albert followed Chaim out the back door of the shop, across a broad alley, and to the back door of the embassy structure. He was greeted by an attractive young woman. "Mr. Lawson, welcome to the Israeli Embassy. The prime minister will be on the line soon, and would like to have a brief word with you. Follow me, please."

She led them to a conference room. They took seats at a table upon which sat a phone.

"Albert, what a pleasure it is to speak with you again, after all these years," said the prime minister over the speaker.

"Mr. Prime Minister. The pleasure's all mine," replied Albert.

"It appears we have been able to keep our part of the bargain. I wanted you to hear from me directly how delighted we are. We wish you many blessings in the future. And, of course, we are ready to see whether and how you can now fulfill your obligation to us. During her debriefing, Mary Catherine assured us she knows where the art is. But she has refused to say where until she's reunited with her children. We quite understand. So, our agents will escort you both back to the States. I trust you will find this arrangement agreeable."

"Absolutely. Thank you, Mr. Prime Minister. I will forever be in debt to you and your amazing people. I look forward to performing my part of the bargain as soon as possible," Albert said with trepidation.

"Thank you for that. Afterward, you must visit me in Jerusalem. Shalom for now."

"I would love that. Shalom, Mr. Prime Minister."

The young woman reappeared. "Mr. Lawson, follow me please."

Albert's legs trembled as he walked. She led him to a door on the second level. "In this room, sir." She smiled, turned and departed, leaving him alone to open the door.

CHAPTER EIGHTEEN

In the static minute during which Jack examined the business card, his mood oscillated like a fan blowing scorching air. In the tumult of his mind, he entertained betrayal, a threat, relief, anger, disillusionment, intrigue, and potential secrets to which he was not privy. He grasped for clarity and logic, rethinking the events of the past few days, wondering why, if his father knew Macon Jones, he had not told him so. *A fellow named Macon Jones wants to hunt Lawson Preserve.* He remembered the sheriff's odd dismissal of the video and how he seemed to endorse Jones as a man to be trusted. His dad's sudden and mysterious trip to France now puzzled him even more than at first. Everyone knew something ... except him. Uncertainty bayed his brain like a hog stopped cold by dogs. That's when he realized the piano was silent, and Macon Jones was standing in the study.

He looked up from the card he held. His eyes met Macon's. And Macon's eyes descended to the card between Jack's fingers.

"Have you ever met my dad?" he asked Macon.

"Can't say that I have. Why?"

"This is your business card. I found it here in Dad's desk."

Macon shrugged. "Maybe someone gave him my card."

"Why would someone give him your card?" Jack's eyes flashed and his voice hardened as he stared at Macon, sick and tired of games. Macon shrugged again. Jack stood up. He placed his hands left and right on his beltline with the fingers of his right hand resting on Old Betsey's deer-antler handle. He sidestepped to the corner of the desk.

"I'd like some straight answers. The car at our guesthouse has a Virginia license plate. Your card has a Virginia address, too."

Macon took note of Jack's body language. "Okay, relax. You're going to have to trust me. I don't know everything. But I'll tell you what I do know. I've been hired as a subcontractor to provide security at Lawson Preserve until further notice. I'm your bodyguard."

"Security? Why?"

"Your family is under a serious threat. That's what the other night was all about. The dudes that landed in the boat from the river were terrorists, not drug dealers."

"How do you know this?"

"It's my job to know."

"The men in the video who took them out?"

"My guys," Macon said.

"Does this have anything to do with my dad's sudden trip to France?"

"I don't know why your dad went to France. But I do know your sister is away for her protection. She also has a bodyguard."

"Why are we threatened?"

"You have something they want."

"What?"

"That's not something I needed to know. All I know is, the threat is serious and real, and I've been authorized to use deadly force, if necessary, to protect these grounds and your family. That's what I know."

Jack paused. "The guy out back, Phelps?"

"He works for me."

"Are there others?"

"Yes, but they're in the shadows."

"Who hired you?"

"I can't tell you that at this time. You should know soon enough ... when the threat abates."

"When will the threat abate?"

"I don't know."

"So, you *have* met my dad?"

"Negative."

"You don't have any idea how he came by your card?"

"I suspect my clients gave it to him."

"And you can't say who your clients are?"

"That would violate my contract. They'll tell you when the time is right."

"Whose side is the sheriff on?" Jack asked.

"I don't know. That's why I suggested we not show him the video from the airfield. I would rather do my job without involving local authorities. They only muck things up. We never should have reported the incident to begin with. I had hoped to remain under cover."

Without taking his eyes off Macon, Jack slipped his phone from his pocket, punched a number and held the phone to his ear. On the seventh ring, Albert answered.

"Hi, Dad. How's your trip so far?" Jack listened as his dad explained all was good. "Things have been nuts here. I'll fill you in when you get home. I'm standing in your study looking at a guy named Macon Jones with Jones Global. He says he's providing security for us for a while. You know anything about this?" Jack listened. "Yes, sir. Yes, sir. Okay. That's all I needed to know. Have a safe trip home. You, too. Bye." He relaxed.

"So?" Macon asked.

"He said you're legitimate. But told me not to ask him questions he can't answer yet. He said he would have news for me when he gets home. It seems no one can answer my questions," Jack muttered. "I wish I knew what was going on."

"I'm glad you made the call. It's not fun keeping secrets. Friends?" Macon asked, extending his hand to Jack.

"Friends," Jack replied, shaking Macon's hand. "So, what's Phelps's job?"

"He's my forward observer, so to speak. We have eyes in the sky, so we saw those clowns coming. Phelps alerted my operators while he was still en route. Then he arranged for air support."

"So, is that why you flew the drone over the house?"

"A miscalculation on my part. I really didn't expect to catch the action. I knew my guys were in place and could handle it. You, my primary responsibility, were with me," Macon replied.

"If my family had been here, and your guys hadn't, what do you think the result would have been?"

"You would have been tortured to death. The house would have been torn to pieces and burned to the ground with y'all in it," Macon replied.

"Who are these people, Make?"

"I can only guess."

"So, guess," Jack pleaded.

"They may be affiliated with an international criminal organization—sort of a global Dark State. We call them slash brokers."

"We?" Jack asked.

"We—the people who resist them."

"Tell me more."

"About the slash brokers?" Macon asked.

"Yeah."

"They're like feral hogs. Hard to hunt. Impossible to get rid of. They've infiltrated the fabric of most countries, operating in the shadows through surrogates. The surrogates don't know with whom they're in league until it's too late. They have ears and eyes everywhere. They're well-financed by criminal operations. By the way, they own a number of US politicians. They're capable of taking down whole countries, and they have. The US is a priority. One of their major goals is to eradicate borders of countries they seek to destroy, facilitating invasions that undermine the economies and cultural identities of a nation. You need look no further than Europe. They leave no stone unturned in their quest to dominate the world. For decades, they've engaged in the sex-slave trade, trafficked in human organs and drugs. They've made billions harvesting body parts from babies in abortion clinics throughout the US and around the world. Recently, the US Senate failed by only a few votes to stop this practice. That's how powerful they are. They own major financial firms, banks, newspapers, casinos, strategic metals industries, technology companies. They're embedded in most of the world's military forces. They portray themselves as angels of light. But they aim to steal, kill and destroy. Their trademark is to accuse their targets of doing what they are, in fact, doing. They're merciless, and they will stop at nothing to increase their power and control the world." Macon paused and took a breath.

Jack dropped to one end of the couch. Macon took a seat opposite him.

"Do they have a leader?"

"Sure. But it's hard to say who. There's an old man approaching one hundred now—amazing he lives—who travels the world like a god. Thinks he is a god."

"Sounds like the Majority Leader," Jack said.

"They're probably kin." Macon smiled.

Jack stared at Macon in disbelief. "Does he have a name?"

"Nicolas." Macon shrugged. "But he's no saint."

"What was your first encounter with them?"

"A while back, a fellow named Stuart Dealier had this same conversation with me. Dealier was underground— dead, if you will—when he approached me for help, and he came to warn me before I ended up dead, too. I was skeptical, at first. But I became a believer. I was working at an Alabama stock brokerage firm. The firm turned out to be a front company for slash brokers and Chinese communists who had infiltrated the US financial system. The Chicoms and the slash brokers were hot and heavy into the international illegal trade in human body parts. Dealier had worked for the same firm but had disappeared. The slash brokers thought Dealier was dead. He had a rare blood type. They search for people with rare blood types. Those organs are in high demand. But Dealier was resurrected. A guy named Jeb Lee published a book called The Slash Brokers. Copies were supposed to have hit newsstands all over the country to coincide with congressional hearings. But the whole matter was suppressed by the media. The media dismissed the story as an outlandish conspiracy hoax by right-wingers. Many believe the slash brokers are embedded in our own agencies along with Chi-com spies. It's believed the Chi-coms were behind the 9/11 attacks. After all, the perpetrators were trained in US flight schools to fly but not land big jets. Agencies of the US government failed to notice—sort of like they fail to notice school shooters who post their intentions on Facebook."

Jack gritted his teeth. "I thought the Saudis were behind the attack in New York."

"Saudi nationals carried out the attack. But some believe others planned and financed it."

"Why the Chinese?" Jack asked.

"Revenge. In May of '99, during a NATO bombing of Yugoslavia, we accidentally destroyed the Chinese Embassy in Belgrade with five US JDAM guided bombs," Macon explained. "This was an alleged mistake. But it made the Chinese furious, as one might expect. They were writhing mad over the *accident* and wanted to impress upon US leadership, in a spectacular way, they wouldn't allow such events to escape judgment. They've been expanding military capabilities ever since—at an alarming rate."

"And the slash brokers? What was their beef?" Jack asked.

"Them? They're the global Dark State. Light infuriates them. And, despite the adverse propaganda you often hear from the media and popular culture about our country, we *are* still the last best hope of the world, the shining city on a hill. That places us in direct conflict with forces of darkness. Any enemy of ours is an ally of theirs."

Jack had been angry and confused. He was now angry but informed. His disposition transformed from inquisitive disquiet to cold-blooded calm.

Macon returned Jack's expressionless stare with his own.

"You're thinking something," Macon said.

"Did you know my mother died in the 9/11 attack?"

"Yes. I was briefed. I'm terribly sorry."

"I wish I had been here," Jack said.

"What do you mean?"

"When those guys landed from the river ..." Jack's voice trailed off.

He stepped to the window and stared out. The river flowed like liquid silver beneath a cloudless blue sky. Trees dressed in fall colors completed a beautiful scene. But Jack saw only ominous, swirling clouds of smoke, fire, and the crashing of towers.

"What'd you do with the bodies?"

"We do our own forensics, after which the bodies are disposed of," Macon replied.

"So, you identify them? Each of them? You'll know who they are? Where they came from? Who they worked for?"

"As best we can, yes," Macon said. "Dark State contractors are not easy to identify. They don't usually carry ID cards. They're often foreign nationals. That makes it tricky. Foreign governments deny involvement."

"Do you guys work with US intelligence?" Macon was silent. Jack turned, and his stormy eyes questioned Macon. "You can't say, right?"

"I've already said too much," Macon replied, then continued, "Jack, I doubt they'll attempt another assault on the house after losing four of their guys. Security into the property and around the house is tight. We can stay here if you like. I'll take your dad's room, if that's okay."

"Sure, whatever," Jack replied, gazing out the window.

"Look, Jack. Don't defeat yourself."

"So, you're a coach, too?" Jack asked, an edge creeping into his voice.

"I know something about what the lust for revenge can do to a man. You still have a lot of life to live. You can make a difference."

Jack looked back at Macon. "Are you making a difference?"

"In my own way, yeah. I think so."

"So, how does one become a contractor?"

"When this is all over, we can talk about that," Macon said. "Meanwhile, why don't you step away from the window for me. Makes me nervous."

Jack complied. "You think they're still out there?"

"One never knows. In my business, we don't stand in front of windows. A competent sniper can kill you from half a mile away."

"This Jeb Lee character, where is he now?"

"He's still out there, writing, researching, living his life," Macon replied.

"His book never took flight?"

"In a big way? No. In smaller ways, yes," Macon said.

"How's that?"

"Soon after the book was published, Lee delivered copies to many US senators and congressmen, including the senator from Alabama."

"You mean ..."

"That's right. The former Attorney General of the United States," Macon said. "Strangely providential, don't you think?"

"You think he actually read Lee's book?"

"I don't know. But, as attorney general, he launched investigations into the harvesting of body parts at US abortion mills. Maybe that's your answer."

"You mean, for all these years, this practice has been known but ignored?" asked Jack.

"For all these years, it has been known, but the political will has not been there to stop it. Again, the slash brokers constitute a powerful force in global politics, and a powerful lobby in Washington. The blood of babies is worth billions. And the slash brokers reward those who bow down to them. They have even owned presidents."

CHAPTER NINETEEN

Jack's phone rang. "Big O. What's up?" Jack stiffened. "No way. You're kidding me, right?" Jack glanced at Macon. "This I've got to see with my own eyes. Right. Okay. I'm on my way!"

"What?" Macon asked.

"That was a friend of the family, Mr. Oliver. He says a handicapped kid nailed the Majority Leader down on the lower forty. Let's go!"

They dashed a few miles in the Rover, exiting the main road. Jack turned into the Pines along a sandy trail and drove several hundred yards.

"There's Big O's pickup," Jack pointed, nearing the blind. "I'll believe this when I see it."

He and Macon jogged toward the blind, hurdling a barbed wire fence, rather than pausing to negotiate it. Big O laughed as they approached the blind. He stood with pride beside the wheelchair where the victorious boy sat grinning up at the men.

Macon glanced at the dead leviathan upon the straw-covered ground, whistled a wistful note, and offered his congratulations to the orange-vested boy. But Jack went straight to the huge carcass and knelt beside it, as if grieving the sudden demise of an old friend. He waved his hand over the animal's grimy body as if administering a last rite. Then, he lowered his hand to the carcass and touched it respectfully. He studied its huge head and long tusks, and noted the missing ear—the white one. He recalled placing the ear in Amos's teeth before lowering his dog into the ground. And he remembered his first encounter with the Majority Leader.

Sun filtered through tall pines, splotching the forest floor, the men and the boy. Birds sang joyfully. At the sight of the massive hog dead on the earth, squirrels chattered and played, as if celebrating its demise. The incongruous scene perplexed Jack. The child's killing of the Majority Leader wasn't trivial or meant to be. Jack felt robbed. He felt Betsy hugging his hip, urging action. But her expertise wasn't needed, perhaps, ever again. A mere child had done his killing for him. Jack slipped his sunglasses off for complete clarity, to better authenticate his dead adversary. He pondered how the Majority Leader's keen intelligence had failed him.

"Maybe," Jack said, shaking his head, "his ego overruled his intellect. But there will be others like him. And smarter. This old hog has fathered thousands of minions to carry on his destructive mission. The Majority Leader is dead, but his evil will live on in the lives of myriad offspring, ranging far and wide."

"That's him, ain't it?" Big O crowed.

"Yep, that's him."

The boy had large brown eyes and locks of dark hair protruding from beneath his orange cap. Bright and handsome, he was fourteen, but small for his age as his infirmity had stunted his growth. Jack liked him immediately and treated him as he would have any other consummate hunter. He stood, walked over to the boy, and offered his hand.

"Jack Lawson."

"I'm Tim," the boy replied, grinning.

"Tim's been wantin' to take his first hog for a while now. So, we decided to make it happen!" Big O gushed.

"And you sure did make it happen! I've been hunting this one without success for a long, long time. Tim, tell me how you took the biggest, smartest, meanest hog in the State of Alabama. I want every detail."

The boy beamed. "Big O and me got here before sunrise and got settled up yonder in the blind. Big O told me to shoot at will. I was ready to take my first hog. But we sat there and sat there, and I didn't think we were ever going to see anything. Then it got a little daylight as the sun started coming up. And I kept watchin' the field. All the sudden, I seen these small pigs darting across the field right to left. It was funny, like they were chasin' each other. Then I seen one grab some corn and keep going toward these woods. So, I got curious about where they were going. I watched through my scope and followed them into the woods. That's when I couldn't believe my eyes. I seen this huge hog tiptoeing through the pines over here like a shadow. I could hardly see him. It was still dark in these trees. The shadow paused. And my cross hairs were right on the mark. Blam! I let 'im have it. He dropped on the spot. I couldn't believe it."

"Good job!" Jack said, patting the boy on the back. He turned to Big O. "Have you called the boys yet?"

"Yeah. They're on the way."

"Let's get some good pictures." Jack smiled at the boy. "This is one for the record books." He turned and sized up the Majority Leader. "I'd say a thousand pounds." He exaggerated—a little—for the boy's benefit.

Other men arrived, including a local reporter. The reporter snapped photographs of the tiny boy behind the massive hog. Others prepared to haul the carcass away.

Jack and Macon walked back to the Range Rover.

"So, what are you thinking, Jack? Happy? Sad? Disappointed it wasn't your kill? What?"

Jack reflected before answering. Macon didn't disturb his thoughts but waited for Jack's reply.

"You know, it's hard to explain. It wasn't supposed to end like this."

"How was it supposed to end?" Macon asked.

"To be honest, I don't know. I always thought I'd be the one to take him, sooner or later, in some dramatic way, like all the others. I don't understand why he bothered to hang around here. It's like he had a personal vendetta against me. He loved to test and torment me, killing my best dog, evading me with great skill, showing me who was boss. He reveled in his deceitfulness. And he toyed with us, the ones who sustained him to hunt him. I guess he knew me better than I knew him. He thought he was invincible. Then along comes this frail child who nails him with one shot. And now, I think he wasn't what he was all cracked up to be. An illusion. It's like his conceit defeated him. God sent a boy to put him in his place. He was just another stupid feral hog. An arrogant Goliath."

Macon observed Jack. "So, all this time, both you and the Majority Leader each thought you were in control. And now?"

"God's in control, I know. God alone. But there's another hog out here in these woods somewhere," Jack said, looking around. "He's even more cunning."

"And does he have a name, too?" Macon asked.

"Satan."

"And so, too, are his days numbered," Macon replied.

"You're speaking metaphorically, of course. But I'm serious, Make. There's a hog out here so crafty that even the dogs can't track him. I've glimpsed him from a tree stand through night-vision goggles. It was scary. Like seeing a ghost. It's as if that particular hog possesses supernatural powers. It has an uncanny ability to sense my presence. To evade my best effort to stalk him. The dogs can't flush him. He's never in the company of other hogs. At least, I've never seen him with others. Aww, I don't know. Maybe it's all in my head."

"And maybe it's not."

"Why do you say that?"

"I know a few things about the latest war fighting tech like drones and robots. I've heard rumors the Army has deployed mechanized hogs—called MH's—on the southern border. These machines look and act like real hogs. But they're controlled remotely. In some cases, from hundreds of miles away. They're using them to stalk and, sometimes, eliminate drug smugglers and other nefarious bad actors approaching our border from Mexico. I wouldn't put it past the government to slip one onto private property and train it in an authentic enemy-combatant environment against a hunter like you. You may think you're hunting Satan, but Satan may be hunting and learning from you," Macon said.

"If what you're saying is true—and I'm beginning to believe anything—I wonder if Satan didn't teach the Majority Leader a few tricks. But what do you mean when you suggest they're training it and that it's learning from me?"

"Artificial intelligence. These machines are super advanced. They're capable of learning, like the computer brains of autonomous cars. A new day has dawned, and the genie is out of the bottle. These machine-warriors will be bloodless, cold-blooded killers, unaffected by emotion. War has changed forever. May God have mercy on the inhabitants of this planet," Macon replied.

The men were silent for a hundred yards. Jack wondered if his bodyguard might know more than he was willing to or could even discuss. He pondered whether Macon could empathize with his peculiar and difficult state of being: trapped in a strange world of his own torturous construction for two decades, tormented by the loss of his mother, deranged with hate for her killers. Jack was beginning to recognize his future was bleak unless he could resolve his complex feelings and find purpose for his life.

"So, how does one become a contractor?" Jack asked.

"It takes years. Hard training. Military contacts. Mutual trust between operators. It's not something you apply for, have an interview, and get hired if you have a sterling personality and a *Who's Who* résumé. And you can't be *meshugga*," Macon said flatly.

Jack paused at the car door and stared across at Macon. "What's that?"

"Meshugga? Crazy."

Jack opened the door and got in the Rover. Macon did the same. They faced each other.

"You think I'm crazy?"

"I'm not a shrink. But I've become pretty adept at psychoanalyzing people. In this work, you have to have a feel for where people are upstairs. I remember working an assignment when my buddy pointed out that my hand was shaking. 'You'll never be a surgeon,' he said. Not that I wanted to be a surgeon, but, funny, he was right. I was shaking like a leaf and didn't even realize it. His life was in my hands and mine in his. It was his way of saying, get a grip, calm down, focus! At first glance, you're a fairly normal guy. But it's easy to see below your surface. Inside, you're a keg of dynamite. Your mind is usually far away, somewhere fighting an ephemeral battle with an enemy always a hand beyond your ability to close with and destroy. If it were not for hunting and killing hogs with your knife, you'd explode. In my view, that state of mind would disqualify you from being hired as a contractor."

Macon paused to allow him to reflect on his words and respond, but Jack remained silent.

Macon shrugged. "People don't always see themselves the way they truly are. It often takes a friend or an enemy to point out weaknesses. I prefer a friend. So, my friend, you have many fine attributes but, until you deal with your past and find a way to put it behind you and move on with your life, you'll remain a mere killer of wild hogs. That would be a shame. Because you have great potential far beyond your hunting skills—potential you may not realize until you've experienced a cleansing transformation of some nature. That could take the form of new responsibility, like a wife and children, or a spiritual awakening, or some form of self-induced catharsis. Transformations aren't easy. And people who will not, or cannot, submit to them invite their own demise." He studied Jack, who stared into the trees. His expression never changed—a sign Macon noted. "Jack, it's possible you may be nearing the end of a long personal transformation now, but don't realize it."

"How's that?" Jack asked, his eyes still fixed on the woods.

"Let me tell you a story. I joined the army on my eighteenth birthday. A week later, I found myself at attention with a drill sergeant in my face calling me every colorful name under the sun. He employed adjectives and metaphors with such ease and skill that he surely must have had a PhD in creative profanity. I can still count the gold teeth in his mouth and feel his spit hitting my face. I braced for what he was going to do to me.

"A horsefly landed on my jaw and chewed my fair skin with license. Blood trickled down my face and neck. I shook in agony. The look on my face must have been stark. The pain the fly inflicted became so intense the DI's tirade became secondary. I wanted to strike the fly. But, despite the pain, I dared not move. The DI raised his right hand as if he was about to slap me upside the head. But he had second thoughts. Officers were watching. Hitting a trainee might have landed the DI in hot water. He lowered his hand back to his side and shouted, 'Jones! Who the blankety-blank gave you permission to feed my blankety-blank horsefly? Gorilla stomps, Jones! Hit it!' I began beating my chest, leaping into the air, falling to my belly, knocking out a pushup, and repeating those movements—what they called gorilla stomps. But in all my physical commotion, the horsefly chewing my face departed. It flew off to chew on some other poor GI. That DI did me a wonderful favor. As I flapped my arms in the air and flung myself on the ground, I was able to move and swat away the hungry fly. When the DI saw the fly was gone, he ordered me back to attention. I glimpsed a smile on his face before he moved on to another recruit. I learned something that day. I realized that, as long as I maintained proper attitude and did what I was told, those DI's would hammer me, but they would also have my back. It was like a spiritual revelation to me. Sometimes, God works like a DI. You've been doing gorilla stomps for a long time, Jack. That can only mean one thing."

"What's that?" Jack asked, looking directly at Macon.

"It means your revelation, when it comes, will be life-altering."

CHAPTER TWENTY

A cool, northwestern breeze nipped his face. Stars reflected in the swamp's black water. Jack studied the imitations, then stared into the moonless cavern of the real heavens. He pondered the infinite stars of a tangible universe. The swamp was real, too, he knew. But it would take the light of truth to make the swamp's character perceptible to the naked eye. The nefarious swamp dwellers hunted, fed and, unchecked, grew and multiplied in total darkness within their own treacherous universe. Jack felt a strange affinity for such beings. In a way, he was like them—in the world but not of it. Creatures great and small accepted his presence and granted him space. The swamp dwellers chanted in a cacophony of unique sounds, each telling its own story. But Jack knew they mimicked one another. Swamp news was always the same. Indeed, the swamp, short of being drained, would never change.

An eerie silence followed a loud splash in the blackness. Jack smiled and whispered, "a thousand and one, a thousand and two, a thousand and three, a thousand ..." The deafening chatter resumed with greater volume than before. Jack closed his eyes and reveled in the sounds of the night. He stood motionless for two hours, then unzipped the netting about his hammock and climbed in. A drone hovering above him departed. Macon retrieved the drone, tucked it away and bedded down. From the tree line, Satan observed the unusual actions of the men and considered the abstract logic and strange strategy they employed.

Song birds ushered in the dawn. A lone, squawking heron glided over Jack's island getaway. He arose, broke down his hammock and tossed it in his small boat. He stood and watched the wetland's transformation at the sun's rising. The air was cold, precipitating a slight mist that hovered over the warm marsh.

Macon leaned against the Range Rover and watched Jack push off and slowly paddle toward the road. Once he reached the shore, Jack secured the boat to a stake and walked toward the SUV, noticing Macon's presence. "Morning," Macon called to him.

"Morning," Jack replied.

"You hungry?"

"Yeah."

"Me too. Let's get some breakfast."

"How did you know where to find me?"

"Your friend Buck suggested you might be out here. I tried not to disturb you. But your safety is my mission, you know. You didn't make my job easy, slipping away without a word."

They got in the Rover. Jack started the engine. "Sorry about that. I needed to get away by myself and think."

"Sure. No harm done. Do you know how long you've been out there?" Macon asked.

"Not really."

"Three days."

Jack shrugged.

"So talk to me, Jack."

"I've been thinking about what you said. You're right. I need a change."

Macon shifted in his seat. "Jack, change is temporary. But transformation is permanent. It's transformation you need. By the way, where's Betsy?"

"Huh?"

"You're not wearing Betsy," Macon observed, nodding at Jack's hip. "That's a good start."

They drove back to Brynhild. Macon built a fire and cooked breakfast while Jack showered and changed clothes. When Jack returned, Macon handed him a steaming cup of coffee and a plate of hot eggs with all the trimmings. They ate with gusto and watched the news. The anchor was reporting the shocking recovery of priceless art from a vault in Switzerland—art stolen from German Jews by the Nazis during World War II.

Macon refilled Jack's cup. "Feeling a little better?" he asked.

"Yeah. That was outstanding. You could make a living as a short order cook if you ever tire of being a contractor."

Macon smiled. "I'll keep that in mind."

"Tell me again your theory about how this transformation business works?"

"Like I said, I'm no shrink. But here's my humble take on the subject. The dual requirements of transformation are motivation and proper attitude. What motivates you to transform?"

Macon muted the TV and studied Jack's large, calloused hands, waiting for Jack to reflect and gather his thoughts.

Jack spoke in earnest. "Fear, I think. Fear I'm going to end up being humiliated like the Majority Leader, and miss all the things in life that matter in the process. I've been killing hogs for twenty years. Frankly, I'm tired of it. But it's who I've become. It's what's expected of me. Gosh. I'm internationally famous for it. Pretty sad, huh? A thirty-four-year-old single guy, living with his dad and little sister, killing wild hogs with dogs and a knife as if there's no greater calling in life."

Macon shook his head. "No, I wouldn't say it's sad to have renown and reputation as a hunter. And this vast preserve is much more than a home. It's a calling. Lots of guys would envy your skills and accomplishments and lifestyle. But remember this, if you're concerned about what other people think about you, you'll forever be trying to be the person you think they want you to be, rather than being the person you are."

"So, who am I?"

"Maybe that's a truer motivation—to discover what God's purpose is for the real Jack Lawson. And to do that, you must become vulnerable to His way of thinking, surrender to His will, and be transformed by the renewal of your mind. Jack, you can kill hogs till the devil becomes an ice sculpture, but that's not going to change the past. But with God, all things are possible. He's waiting for you to trust Him, even in the painful things of life. When you do, you'll also have the proper attitude. That's where transformation begins. That's when you'll start serving others and forget about yourself. I know. I've been there."

Jack watched flames leaping in the fireplace and contemplated Macon's words. Then he spoke with less sadness, as if having shifted gears in his mind. "Isn't it interesting how all of a sudden the stories about me and hogs have vanished? There's no mention of it on TV. Have you noticed?"

"Yes, I have. You're yesterday's headline now. It was a lot of baloney and hysteria to begin with."

"I know. But for a while it seemed like the whole world was in a panic about hog hunting. And now—nothing! Blackout. It's crazy. If the world is so upset about it, where are the activists now? Will it all explode again at some point? Or is it over?"

"I think it's over. These days, media focus shifts like wind direction over the ocean. But beneath the surface, there's real news of great importance that goes unreported. The media masters feed us distractions to keep our eyes from news that matters. And from truth. But the media masters—they know what's happening. They know," Macon said.

"And who are the media masters?"

"The media masters? They're the ones who control what is known and what is thought. The masters of delusion. Creators of chaos. And, if we listen to them, we become slaves of delusion."

"But who are they?"

"Ah, you want names? Me, too. But names shouldn't be hard to come up with. Marxists have joked that, in America, the working class is Democrat, the middle class Republican, but the upper class is communist. Internet billionaires own the global media complex and have for years. For some strange reason I'll never understand, they despise the free enterprise system that birthed them."

Jack sighed. He thought about Carla Frederick and the *World News.*

CHAPTER TWENTY-ONE

A ball cap secured her ponytail in place. She wore a gray Patagonia Nano-Puff jacket, jeans, and slip-on sneakers. Traveling light with a small carry-on, she was incognito—the way she preferred to travel. Carla checked her phone for messages. None. She huffed in confusion and frustration. *Why isn't he returning my calls?* She determined not to call him again. She remained upset over the considerable trouble she had caused him, yet relieved that the 24/7 rehashing of her story had disappeared from news screens. She watched through her sunglasses as frantic travelers scurried by her gate at Atlanta's Hartsfield International.

At first glance, Carla didn't recognize the man approaching with a beautiful woman, walking beside him hand-in-hand. But as they passed near, she studied them and concluded the man was indeed Albert Lawson. She started to stand and speak—but then she hesitated. *Perhaps Albert is over his wife's death and has a girlfriend. But an introduction might be awkward for them both. He might not relish seeing me. His son, after all, won't answer or return my calls.*

As she contemplated the time she and Jack had spent together and certain words that had passed between them, her heart ached for reconciliation. Chances were, she would never see the Lawsons again—a thought that grieved her. As she watched them walk away, she observed the curious presence of two men walking in front of them, and two behind, like escorts or bodyguards. While Lawson and the woman were attired in travel clothes, the men wore dress slacks, blazers, and sunglasses. None of them carried bags. She watched curiously as they disappeared from view.

Maybe she should cancel her flight to New Orleans to surprise a friend and, instead, fly to Alabama and drive to Brynhild. But what might she arrive in the midst of? And besides, she hadn't heard from Jack in days. Suppose he'd had a change of heart? How would she be received there? And did her article in the *World News* have anything to do with Albert and his friend having bodyguards?

Her phone rang. She glanced at the screen and rolled her eyes. "Hey, Arlan. I'm about to get on a plane. Can't talk long. What's up?"

"Where are you?"

"Atlanta, why?"

"Sorry, babe. I don't mean to pry. I'm calling to give you a heads up."

"About what?"

"About death threats."

"What? Arlan, get to the point please."

"Someone slipped a note to one of our secretaries on the street."

"And?"

"And it said 'death to Carla Frederick.'"

"Great! So, what did I do to deserve death this time?"

"Who knows? Lots of nuts in the world today. End times, you know. Lawlessness. Gnashing of teeth." Arlan laughed. "Just be careful out there and stay close to family and friends. Keep in touch."

"Sure. Thanks for the warning. Bye."

Carla looked about. *Arlan was right when he said there are lots of nuts in the world today. In the Middle East, death threats, kidnappings, beatings and risk of rape were routine occupational hazards. But this is American soil. Danger should not be an issue.*

But she knew this was no longer the case. American borders leaked like sieves. She had seen the reports of terrorists crossing into the US—reports her organization never printed. And the one place she would feel safe, Brynhild, now seemed off-limits. She wished she knew why.

Carla sighed, turned her phone off, and prepared to board.

Jack dialed her number.

CHAPTER TWENTY-TWO

When Macon and Jack returned from the field, they noticed a new twin-engine plane at the airstrip. Several armed men stood in the open near the house.

"It's okay," Macon said. "I recognize them."

Jack left Macon behind and headed into the house. He strolled into his father's study. Dagny was sitting on the sofa. Another man whom he had seen come and go from Brynhild over the years—a man he had always wondered about—stood as Jack walked in. He assumed the man was his father's business associate. At least, that was the explanation he'd been given over the years.

"Jack," Albert nodded. The lines in his face spoke of the serious nature of the meeting, as if he knew of bad news and regretted to share it. He frowned but then smiled, rubbed his chin, and breathed deeply.

"I have special news. Wonderful news. Please sit down." Albert paused as Jack took a seat on the sofa beside Dagny. "There's no easy way for me to share what I have to tell you. But here goes.

"I'd like you to meet Chaim Cohen. You may recognize him. He's been a visitor here over the years. Chaim is an Israeli intelligence officer. He's been searching for your mother for twenty years. He's going to brief you and answer your questions. Chaim ..."

Chaim smiled. He looked them in the eyes. "Jack, Dagny. I feel like I know you well."

Jack and Dagny exchanged a look. What was an Israeli intelligence officer doing in Alabama? They nodded to the man, but then pushed forward to the edge of the sofa, giving Albert their complete attention. Jack found his voice first. "What's happened here, Dad?"

Albert cleared his throat. "Your mother didn't die in the 9/11 attacks."

Dagny gasped.

"Sir?" Jack said, as if he had misunderstood.

"She's not dead," Albert repeated.

"Where is she?" Jack's voice rasped.

Albert smiled. "She's here."

And then she walked into the room. Her compassionate blue eyes had faded but were still filled with joy. Lines found the corners of her eyes. Her cheeks had lost their youthful rosiness. Her dark hair was graying and not silky as it had once been. But for a mother resurrected from the dead, she was stunning.

The hugs and tears had slowed, but not stopped. And probably wouldn't stop for a while.

Mary Catherine, who still had one arm around Jack, turned to Dagny. She took Dagny's face in her hands and smiled. "So often I've wanted to do this over the years." She stroked Dagny's hair and beheld her daughter like a little girl would study a new doll. Then she turned back to Jack. "We have so much catching up to do."

"What happened?" Jack finally asked.

Chaim Cohen stood. "I think that's my cue. The story begins with your grandfather—the man you called 'Pop'—at the end of World War Two. He was stationed in Munich after the German surrender, and he stumbled upon a cache of valuable art in a bombed-out building. He brought that art home with him, not knowing its worth or where it came from."

"But everyone knows that was just a legend," Dagny said.

"We've all heard there was some war treasure here," Jack seconded her. "But nobody ever believed it."

"It was true," Albert replied, sitting down. "We kept the art in a safe in the attic. It was stored there for years."

"Now wait," Jack said. "I've been in that safe, and I've never seen it."

"One thing at a time," Mary Catherine said. "Let your father continue."

Albert smiled. "Years ago, when the mill was going downhill, Pop met with art appraisers in New York. He wanted to appraise one of the works in hopes of selling it and raising cash to keep the mill alive. The appraisers listened to Pop's story, recognized the art, and explained to Pop how it was confiscated from Jews during the Holocaust. But when Pop realized the nature of the works—not to mention their immense value—he decided it was too risky to try and sell them. He knew once his possession of the art became public, there could be repercussions from the IRS, the German and Israeli governments, and who knows who else. So, he decided to leave it alone. We closed the mill. Pop died. But the secret was out. When the market for these masterpieces exploded, pieces like the one he had shown were selling for millions of dollars."

Mary Catherine reached out and took Albert's hand, smiling. "After that, I had a premonition we were all in danger and decided to take precautions. I meant to tell you, Albert, but never had the chance. I got the idea from a suspense novel I'd read. I knew the art was priceless and didn't want to take any chances we might be forced to open the attic safe by thieves. And the attic was a horrible place to keep it. Can you imagine the house catching fire? I was doing some home repairs anyway. So, I had a fake wall constructed at a machine shop. I installed, caulked and painted it myself while you were on a business trip. It's been in its little hiding place ever since."

"But what does it have to do with you being kidnapped?" Dagny's voice came out as a near-wail.

"We believe that word of the artwork reached the ears of a Middle-Eastern terrorist cell," Chaim said.

"A man, using what turned out to be a false identity, called me," Albert went on. "Inquiring about the art. I refused to discuss it, hung up on him and tried to forget it."

"We believe the call your father received may have been a representative of that cell," Chaim told them. "Rebuffed by your father, these same terrorists kidnapped your mother in New York. The kidnapping occurred the same day she was to have visited your uncle who worked at the World Trade Center. She was held against her will all these years because of art."

Albert shook his head. "After 9/11, I looked in the attic. The art was gone. That's when I realized there was some subterfuge going on."

"You never told us!" Jack cried out. "We could have gotten to her sooner—"

"No." The tempo in Albert's discourse increased. "I cannot begin to tell you how many times I've wanted to tell you. But for reasons I think you'll appreciate, I simply could not."

"Your father was convinced the two events—your mother's disappearance and the disappearance of the art—were related," Chaim Cohen said. "He didn't know how, and he didn't know where she could be, or even if she was alive. But he believed Israel would help him—if he could convince the Israeli government of the possibility of recovering millions of dollars' worth of stolen Jewish art. His hope became a reality when the prime minister listened to his story. The Tel Aviv Museum of Art got involved. They tasked me with finding your mother and retrieving the art. We probed and listened, and we began to hear things." He grinned. "I hope you children know your mother is a genius. She never lost her head. Over the years, her captors became lenient with her. She charmed them and outfoxed them. She baited her captors and played them for the foolish thieves they are."

Mary Catherine's voice was careful, as if considering each word before she allowed it to escape. "I convinced them the works had been locked in a Swiss bank vault. And that no one, not even I, could access the vault until the end of the statute of limitations on possession of stolen Nazi art. I told them my claim to the art was the subject of a legal document placed under seal. That I was the sole person—the key, so to speak—to break the seal and repossess the art. If I were treated well and my family left alone, I pledged to take them to Switzerland and get the art—after the statute of limitations expired. If anything happened to me—or to any member of my family—the art would remain in the vault. Forever."

"They believed her," Chaim said, sounding almost as if the triumph belonged to him. "Many European art thieves awaited the same event. But after many years, the terrorists got lazy. They even allowed her to go out in Paris—always, of course, under heavy guard. They dressed her in a burqa, until the French banned women from covering their faces in public. One day she passed a note, written in French, to a shop clerk. The clerk turned the note over to the French police, who in turn contacted the American Embassy. The note named Albert Lawson in Alabama and gave her location in Paris, a flat over a shop on the *Rue de la Paix*. At first, authorities thought it was a case of sex-trafficking.

They contacted your father about the note. He contacted us. But the cell kept moving her around within Paris's terrorist enclaves where the police were not permitted to go. By the time authorities got around to raiding the flat, she was gone. The trail went cold."

"Now do you see?" Albert's eyes pleaded with his children to understand. "Every thread I grasped seemed to run out. How could I raise your hopes only to dash them again?"

Jack looked doubtful. "But I could have ..."

"No." Dagny seemed to get a little smaller. "Dad must've been heartbroken. Bad enough it happened to him—he's our dad, and he wanted to protect us from that. I get it."

"I knew you were wise beyond your years," said Mary Catherine.

"But why her in the first place?" Jack demanded. "Why not Dad, or even me?"

"Her appearance in New York on 9/11 provided them the perfect cover for their crime, Jack." Cohen shrugged. "They figured your dad would do anything to get her back. That she was the key to obtaining the art. But she convinced them your father didn't know where the art was. She told them pestering your dad would only risk exposing themselves and blowing the possibility of ever acquiring the art. She played her best hand.

"The terrorists had a huge incentive to keep her assumed death undisturbed. But your mother dealt with her situation brilliantly. She was at home in Paris, though under constant surveillance. To her captors, she was worth—perhaps half a billion dollars. She was their *L'argent clé*, their key to money. They would have killed her as soon as they realized she had deceived them. In fact, they may have killed some of you." He looked around, letting that thought sink in.

"We continued to pursue leads," he said. "An art appraiser in a Paris café overheard a man bragging about

166

a stash of Jewish art worth millions of Euros. The man spoke of a woman he called *L'argent Clé*—Key Money. The appraiser contacted Art Curator Ariel Akiba in Tel Aviv. It was like manna from heaven. Our agents found that man. He led us to your mother."

"They rescued me just in time," Mary Catherine said. "Chaim, I can never repay you."

"Maybe not." Chaim chuckled and gave her a wink. "But restoring our lost art would go a long way toward it."

Mary Catherine laughed along with him. "You're right. Enough suspense. Albert, will you open the safe—the large one behind the bookcase?"

"But you said it was a fake wall—"

"Trust me, my love."

Albert shook his head. He walked over and pressed a wall panel. The bookcase released from the wall. He pushed the bookcase back against the adjacent wall and flipped a light switch inside the small room. The others watched as Albert worked the combination lock.

Mary Catherine whispered something to Jack. He nodded and left the room.

Albert pressed down on the safe's handle and opened the large steel door without fanfare. He glanced inside and lowered his head. He stepped back and motioned for others to look. They saw guns, ammunition, personal documents, but nothing more. No art.

"Remove everything from the safe," Mary Catherine said.

Albert stared at his wife, speechless.

"All the guns, the shelves, everything," she added.

Albert glanced at Chaim, whose rough face revealed only intrigue and intensity.

"I may need some help with these shelves," he said, as Jack reentered the room with a pair of pliers in hand.

"Jack, please help your dad remove the shelves," Mary Catherine said.

Soon the safe was a hollow shell. Mary Catherine took the pliers from Jack and smiled at Albert. "Thank you, dear. Well done."

She dropped to her knees inside the safe and pried loose a small tab of metal on the bottom left corner of the rear wall. Gripping the tab and pulling hard, she opened a small door in the back surface. She reached through the opening and nodded.

Scooting back from the safe, she stood and faced them. "The safe has a fake back wall. You'll find all the art behind it."

"They've been right there all this time," Albert cried. "I thought they had been stolen! I've wondered all these years where they could possibly be."

"Had you known, this story may have had a different ending," Mary Catherine replied. "My captors were capable of great brutality. Had they suspected the art was here at Brynhild, or had you tried to deliver the art in exchange for me, the outcome may have been dreadful for both of us. They might have killed me and no one would ever have been the wiser. I was thought to be dead anyway. But it's all in the past now. We have the future. For that, we can be grateful."

"She's right," Chaim said. "As you know, Albert, there have been attempts ..." Albert raised his hand, and Chaim's mouth clamped shut.

Jack removed the fake wall and stood clear, allowing Chaim access.

The Israeli removed and examined the paintings one at a time. "Remarkable. Well preserved!"

"Are they what you were hoping for?" Albert asked.

"I'm hardly an expert. Just a delivery boy. But, yes, I recognize a couple as Chagall's work. If these are authentic, and I have every reason to believe they are, then this portfolio's priceless. This calls for champagne!" He smiled. "I happen to know there is some chilling in the kitchen. Shall we?"

CHAPTER TWENTY-THREE

Macon joined them in the kitchen. Albert introduced Mary Catherine and was explaining the miracle of her presence as armed Israeli agents entered with special containers. They transferred the paintings to them, and upon Chaim's command, departed at a trot. Minutes later, an airplane roared over the house.

The phone in the study rang and Jack left the room. When he returned, Albert observed his son's face.

"Son, is everything okay?"

"No, sir. Carla's father called from Virginia. He said he received a call from her editor in Los Angeles yesterday warning of a death threat against her. She was on her way to visit a friend in New Orleans but never showed. He wanted to know if she might be here at Brynhild."

Chaim placed his champagne down and turned to Jack. "Pardon me. You're speaking of the *World News* journalist who wrote the story about you, right?"

"Yes, sir. Why?"

"She wrote a story a while back that was picked up in Europe. The story speculated about an obscure, albeit dangerous, well-funded, terrorist cell our intelligence indicated had entered the EC through Turkey, posing as Syrian refugees. Her story described them as 'raising murder to an art—an art that was the key to their money.'

We investigated her because the use of all three words, *art, key, money,* in the same line, set off bells and whistles with our algorithm. But we concluded that it was just a coincidence. Omar may have felt otherwise."

Mary Catherine placed her hand over her mouth. "Oh! I remember overhearing Omar ranting about a journalist who used those very words. He took Carla to be a mysterious spy sending a message. But to whom and for what purpose, he didn't know. He wanted to interrogate her and learn whose side she was on and to whom she was conveying intel about the art."

Macon's body language shifted from guest and casual observer to security contractor. "Who's Omar?"

"He's one of the ringleaders who kidnapped me. It's possible Omar thinks he has connected the dots, that Carla Frederick was somehow connected with the rescue operation that freed me. They kept me alive all these years and thought they were so close to acquiring the art. Then in one week they lost me, lost the art ... and their cell was exposed. They must be blind with anger. This makes them more dangerous. Omar is vindictive. He will seek revenge however he can on whomever he can. Carla may be in grave danger but have no clue why or from what."

"I'm on it," Macon stated. He dashed from the room, Jack on his heels. Macon barked orders as they rushed out the door.

Albert and Mary Catherine turned to Chaim.

"Just as I thought all of this had come to a close ..." Albert said.

Mary Catherine drew close to Albert, took his arm and squeezed it. Dagny joined them.

"Jack will find her, Daddy," Dagny said.

Chaim took a deep breath. "I'm sorry, my friend. Is Jack involved with the young lady?"

"Let's just say we're both fond of her," Albert replied. "Despite her story."

"But let's not jump to conclusions," Chaim said. "We'll see what Macon comes up with and go from there. Our resources are at your disposal. Macon will stay in touch with me, and we'll help any way we can." He raised his glass in a toast. "To his mercies."

"To his mercies," they chorused.

Chaim stepped closer, facing Albert and Mary Catherine. They locked moist eyes. "My friends," Chaim began, "this has been a long journey for you. I must go now. Please know that you will forever be in my prayers. Do not hesitate to call on me if I may ever be of assistance. Next year in Jerusalem?"

"Next year in Jerusalem." Albert smiled. They exchanged hugs. Chaim departed the house and walked to his car where a driver waited. He glanced up at the cloudless sky, said a prayer, and they drove away.

Macon and Jack hurried back into the kitchen.

"She never made her scheduled flight," Jack said.

Macon stared at his phone. Text messages filled the screen. "She took a different flight to Shreveport and rented a car there. The rental agency has tracked the car to an area northwest of the airport."

"What's there?" Albert asked.

Macon struck his left palm with his right fist. "Nothing much. A Texas state park. That concerns me. No one's heard from her. She's not answering her phone. Jack and I are flying out there. My man's filing a flight plan now. We'll be in touch."

"Macon, shouldn't we call Shreveport authorities and have them look for her?" Albert asked. "She may need immediate assistance."

"Mr. Lawson, we have no reason to suspect she's in trouble. But if Omar's people are involved, I'd rather maintain the element of surprise. If she's alive, we'll get her back. We'll call the park authorities. They should be able to tell us if she's there with someone or alone. Chances are, she just decided to visit the park. Who knows?"

"I'll grab a dog and the scarf she gave me. Meet you at the plane, Make. I'll be in touch, Dad," Jack said, darting away.

Jack arrived at the plane with a leashed Catahoula leopard dog.

Macon took one look at the canine and asked, "Does he howl when on a scent?"

"Negative. He's trained to track with stealth, point, and if signaled, attack. He won't like being cooped up in the plane. But once on the ground, he'll be eager to work."

"What's his name?"

"Patton."

Macon smiled. "He must be one fierce dog."

They were airborne in minutes.

CHAPTER TWENTY-FOUR

CADDO LAKE STATE PARK, TEXAS

The middle-aged park ranger gave Carla the once-over. "Welcome, Miss. May I help you?"

"Do you have a cabin?"

"Sure do. How will you be paying?"

Carla handed the ranger her credit card. "My card. I'd like to rent the smallest one you have."

"How many nights?"

"One."

"I'll need a driver's license and some general information." He slid a form toward her and went about running the card.

As Carla filled out the form, he asked, "Are you traveling alone?"

Carla bristled. She gave him a hard look. "Why do you ask?"

"Just wondered. We rarely have young ladies show up here alone."

"Is that a problem?"

"No, ma'am. Have you ever been here? Are you familiar with the park?"

"Passing through. I read about the park. Sounded like I'd enjoy seeing it and could unwind." She paused from the form and watched for his reaction.

He smiled and nodded. His eyes were kind and conveyed no mischief. She relaxed.

"It's a special place, for sure. But not without hazards. Watch for gators if you go near the bayou. Stay clear of them."

"Don't worry," she replied.

"There's a boat tour you can take. That's the best way to see the sights. You can register for it here. Would you like to do that now?"

"When does the tour depart?"

"In the morning. Nine-thirty."

"Hmm ... I'll sleep on it."

"Okay. If you decide to go, drop by here in the morning about nine. It shouldn't be crowded."

She pushed the form back and handed him her license. He took the ID, placed it against the form and made a couple of notes.

"You'll be in cabin four. None of the other cabins are occupied. You'll have the whole place to yourself. Do you have everything you need?"

"Not exactly. Is there a store nearby that might have groceries?"

He handed her a short list. "Here's what we have."

She took the list and shrugged. "Thanks. Are we done?"

He handed her a pamphlet, key, her ID and credit card. "These are the rules and a map to your cabin. Your key. The gate closes at nine."

"Thank you." She turned toward the door and was about to exit when he spoke up.

"A man called earlier asking if we had seen a young woman here. The description he gave fits you pretty good."

She stopped cold, turned and glared at him. "I beg your pardon?"

"Yes, ma'am. Would that be you?"

"I don't know," she replied. "Did he give a name or say why he was calling?"

"I'm sorry. I didn't pay close attention or take notes because my answer was 'no.' I told him we haven't had anyone fitting his description. Not on my watch. And definitely not today. Until you walked in, that is. Our policy is to not give out information about guests."

"That's a good policy. Did he ask for me by name?"

"I ... I ... don't really remember."

"Did he have an accent?"

"An accent? Hmm, I don't think so."

"And he gave no name?"

"He did but ... wait! I think it was Jones. I remember thinking, my brother-in-law is a Jones."

"A first name, too?"

"Uh ... uh ... I'm sorry. I don't recall," he said, scratching his chin.

"Well, thank you. It's probably a coincidence. Someone looking for someone, but not me. I'm not expecting company and no one knows I'm here." Carla realized she had volunteered too much. "I mean, except for my boyfriend in Shreveport. He may come out later," she lied.

"I see," the ranger replied, resuming his duties.

That was dumb. Should I tell him there's a threat on my life? She walked to her car. *Perhaps it's too much of a coincidence.* She formulated a new plan, paying close attention to park visitors she passed en route to her cabin.

A scattering of pines enclosed the small, charming cabin. A combination of logs and stones adorned its quaint entrance. It looked like a hobbit's house. *This is the last place in the world anyone would expect to find me. So serene, remote, perfect. And now I must leave ... before I'm found. And by whom?* She decided to stay until dark, then ease away.

Since leaving Atlanta, she had neglected to reactivate her phone, determined to be unavailable until she was ready. She contemplated what she had seen in Atlanta— Albert Lawson, the woman, the presence of security with them. Arlan's call warning her of a death threat weighed on her. She sat on the steps of the cabin in the middle of nowhere. *My notion of a peaceful respite from the world has been shattered.* She unlocked the door, stepped inside and looked around. She turned on a light, then exited the cabin, locked the door, and walked outside, strolling to a bench. She took a seat and tried to relax. *Am I being ridiculous, too cautious, paranoid?* She strolled beyond the cabin toward the lake, vexed by an eerie feeling of being watched. Being followed.

She intended only a brief walk to clear her mind. Not far along the trail to the bayou, she turned to go back. She saw a man in a black hoodie and dark glasses following at fifty yards. The man stopped on the trail and gawked at her. She froze and struggled to control fear. They stood staring at each other. Neither moved. Then the man continued toward her. She backed up, turned and ran.

Darkness descended. Swamp creatures began to sing and chatter. Carla obsessed with the sound of her shoes striking earth and the noise of her panting. The trail veered east. She glimpsed the surreal image of swamp gleaming in the vanishing light, juxtaposed against cypress trees and ghostly, dripping moss. She glanced back. Didn't see him. But she knew he was there. Closing on her. She sprinted forward. But the swamp was dead ahead. She darted off the trail into the darkening woods. Vines and branches lashed her. She tripped on a root and fell face-first into the muck. A large bird screeched in protest and flapped away like sheets in a tempest.

The man stopped on the trail and peered into the woods, then he jogged toward her.

Carla struggled up and sprinted deeper into the woods, dodging trees, stumps and vines. She stopped for breath and looked back, watching for movement, glimpsing his silhouette.

The man stopped, too. Thick trees and darkness obscured visibility.

"Carla!"

She threw a stick into the woods. It struck a tree and snapped. The silhouette moved toward the sound. She stayed low and skulked away in the opposite direction, toward where she thought the trail might be.

"Carla!"

Her heart pounded. But the voice sounded farther away than before. She squatted behind a large tree, shoes descending into muck. She waited, listened, tried to calm herself, daring not to peek. Pressing against the oak, she made herself small.

"Carla! Come to me!"

The moon sojourned on the opposite side of earth, allowing blackness to engulf the cold woods. The raucous, deafening noise of a thousand critters filled the air.

Again, his voice split nature's chatter like the ringing of a bell. "I won't hurt you, Carla. Come now. I know you're here. Trust me. It will be better for you if you will come to me. Do we have to play hide and seek?"

Carla ignored him and kept still.

"It's okay. I like games."

The voice sounded more distant. *Darkness is my friend. But I'm lost and don't know which way to go.* She prayed. And as she prayed, courage surged within her. Somewhere in the distance behind her, a car door slammed. She rolled away from the tree and crawled on all fours toward the sound, hoping to put as much distance as possible between herself and her stalker.

"Carla!"

She crawled farther, faster, peering through the woods toward the sound she had heard but seeing no lights, only nearby trees and darkness beyond. She fought the urge to run but continued crawling, not realizing the trail she sought lay beneath her hands and knees. She reentered the woods on the other side, crawled twenty yards and rolled into a ball against yet another large oak with low accessible limbs for climbing. But she didn't think to look up.

Macon's special-ops man had rented a car and had it parked by the hanger at Shreveport Regional. Within minutes of landing, Macon, Jack and Patton were en route to Caddo Lake State Park. They sped along Highway 80 West, then due north, arriving in thirty minutes. The gate was open but the ranger station was closed, with no one in sight. They parked and killed the lights.

"You ever seen a darker night?" Macon asked.

"Yeah."

"I haven't. The rental agency said they tracked the car here. Funny, the ranger I spoke with denied seeing a young woman here alone. That bugs me," Macon said.

"Me too. Let's see if Patton agrees."

Jack gave Patton the scent and released him. But the hound ran in circles.

"It's not likely she's tent-camping. Let's check out the cabins," Macon said.

They drove farther. At cabin four, they found a compact car fitting the description of the rental. Patton sniffed straight to the door. They knocked and peered through the windows. A lamp filled the small cabin with light, but no one was there. Patton ran circles around the house, sniffing the steps, the car, a bench. Then he lunged, attempting to run. Jack held the leash firmly. They strapped on night vision goggles and trotted away, with Patton's nose to the ground.

Carla shivered in the chilly air and fought to keep her wits. Wet muck filled her shoes, exacerbating her misery. A limb from a distant tree snapped and crashed to the ground. An armadillo scurried by, rustling leaves and twigs, sending her nerves into convulsions. She checked herself, reasoning, *an animal*. Neither her presence nor the presence of any other human alarmed the critter. A good sign. But she stayed put, quiet and still. She considered he might be doing the same close by. She closed her eyes, took measured breaths and prayed.

A dot of red light danced on the tree she hugged. The dot zigzagged over the murky ground and upon trees beyond. Carla was oblivious to the dot's dance. But the sound of footfalls terrified her. She opened her eyes and realized they had adjusted to the dark. As had his. She closed them again, continued to pray, and prepared for the worst.

"Carla?"

Carla trembled but kept silent. The speaker took another step. Stopped. Stepped closer. Stopped. Terror gripped her. But she managed to look up. The man's appearance was like that of an alien being. He wore night vision goggles and held a handgun with a laser sight.

He knelt beside her. "Carla, it's Jack. Jack Lawson. Are you okay?"

Jack pushed the goggles from his face.

She remained silent for a second, in shock, whimpering, "Jack? Jack!" She slumped into his arms.

"It's okay. I've got you. Can you walk?" he whispered.

"I think so. Someone's after me. He may still be here, Jack. I thought ..."

He placed a finger over his lips and whispered, "It's okay. Let's go."

He helped her up and held her close as they trudged over the moist ground. Macon waited on the trail, holding tight Patton's leash.

Patton continued to point.

Seeing Macon Jones for the first time, Carla held back.

"He's with me. Macon Jones."

"Jones?" Carla repeated.

"Yeah," Jack whispered.

"The ranger said a man named Jones called here ..."

"That was me," Macon replied, scanning the woods. "I flew Jack here. We'll explain everything later. Let's go."

Patton looked toward the swamp and growled.

They stooped low. Jack replaced his goggles and scanned the woods. A man moved between trees in the distance. He disappeared behind a tree, reemerged, covered new ground in a random pattern. Vanished. Reappeared. The man moved like a hungry carnivore on the prowl.

"Carla, stay here with Macon." Jack unleashed Patton. "Patton. Bite."

Patton dashed into the night. The woods filled with vicious growling and agonizing wails. Jack reached the fray in seconds and pulled Patton off the man. He reattached Patton's leash, and tied the loose end to a small tree. Patton continued to lunge.

The man scrambled up and snapped open a switchblade. He thrust forward, aiming to plunge the blade into Jack's chest. Jack jumped back out of range, one hand on Betsy. The man advanced again in a slashing maneuver directed at Jack's throat. Jack outed Betsy and blocked his swing, slicing the man's hand tendons. The fight was over. Unable to grasp his knife, the man fled.

Jack released his dog. "Patton, bite."

The dog caught the man in the buttocks, shredding his pants. Jack caught up and restrained Patton again. Freed from the dog, the man continued to run. Jack and Patton pursued him to the edge of the swamp. But the delirious man careened into the water, thrashing about. Jack watched in horror as two alligators competed for the fresh meat, yanking Carla's stalker below the watery bisque.

Jack backtracked, searching for the man's knife. Patton sniffed straight to the cloth he'd ripped from the attacker's trousers. Close by, Jack found a billfold. And farther along, the knife. Jack closed the knife and stuck it in his pocket. He examined the contents of the billfold. A driver's license. Cash. A photo of Carla. A photo of Dagny.

Jack and Patton returned to find Macon and Carla still crouched on the trail.

"What the heck happened out there?" Macon asked.

"He decided to go swimming with alligators."

"Who was he?" Carla asked.

"Just another swamp creature. Let's get out of here!" Jack whispered.

They hurried back to the cars and raced away.

At Shreveport Regional, they returned the rental cars, boarded Macon's plane and were soon airborne.

Jack turned to Carla. "I've got much to share with you, Carla. But not now. Rest. There's a clean room and hot shower waiting for you at Brynhild."

Jack texted his dad:

JACK: We have Carla. Rough night. But all's good. Don't wait up. No boisterous greeting. She needs a shower, bed, and rest. We'll meet and greet tomorrow.

CHAPTER TWENTY-FIVE

Everyone clapped when Carla strolled into the kitchen. She recognized the attractive lady she had seen with Albert at the airport, but had no clue of the relationship or circumstances. Confusion, if not embarrassment, reigned in her head, as if she'd been guilty of interloping and bad timing.

"Carla!" Dagny yelled.

They surrounded and hugged her as if she were a lost puppy, found. The attractive lady was reserved, yet smiling, watching, waiting for an appropriate introduction.

"We thought you were in danger!" Dagny shouted. "We were worried to death! Where have you been?"

"Oh my gosh. I didn't know I was missing. I was leaving Atlanta for New Orleans. But my flight was overbooked. The airline called for a volunteer to give up a seat. At the last minute, I changed my mind and caught a flight to Shreveport. I wanted to get away by myself and think. There's a Texas state park near Shreveport called Caddo Lake. I rented a car and drove there. It's a beautiful, mysterious place I had read about. But I don't ever want to go back."

"Why? What happened?" Dagny asked.

Carla turned and searched Jack's eyes. He smiled. "We can talk about that later, Dag. Let's just say Caddo Lake reminded her of Lawson Preserve. She got homesick and wanted to come here instead."

"These guys turned up out of thin air like knights in shining armor," Carla gushed. "And here I am. I just hope I'm not intruding."

"Not at all!" Albert said. "In fact, you're just in time for the party!" Albert took Mary Catherine's hand and pulled her close. "Carla, I have someone very special I'd like you to meet. It's a long, long story, but ... this is my first and only wife, Mary Catherine."

Carla's eyes grew wide and she gasped. "What? But ..."

"And that's what we all thought," Albert said. "Miracles really do happen!"

Mary Catherine gave Carla a hug then looked deep into her eyes as a mother would. "It's such a pleasure to meet you, Carla. I'm so relieved to see you, and I look forward to getting to know you. We were all concerned. This is a double blessing for me."

Carla's eyes filled with tears. "Oh my gosh. For me, too. I'm stunned. I don't know what to say." She looked at Jack with questioning eyes.

Mary Catherine squeezed Carla's hand, glancing at the faces around her. "Please excuse me. I'll be right back."

Carla waited until Mary Catherine had left the room then said, "Jack, why don't you take me for a walk and brief me about recent events."

"Good idea," Albert added. "Meanwhile, let's all just love on Mother. That's what she needs most." He turned to Macon. "Thank you, my friend, for all you've done. I understand your men had a little dust-up while we were away. I'm thankful you guys were here. What are your plans now?"

"We'll continue to hang out here for a day or two until we get new marching orders. I'd like to do some research on this Omar fellow and see if we can get a handle on his location," Macon said.

"Good! Let me know if there's anything at all we can do for you guys—to make your stay more comfortable. Anything at all."

"Thank you, sir." Macon smiled and departed for the guest house.

Jack and Carla strolled beneath the trees where Old Amos rested. "For all these years, we've believed she was dead along with Uncle Jack. But she was being held for ransom. It's hard to believe. Israeli agents left here yesterday. With them was the art that was in our safe. And we didn't know that either. And the same terrorist thug who kidnapped Mom is apparently looking for you now. His name is Omar. He probably thinks you were in on her rescue."

"I had dismissed the death threat. Why in the world would they think I was involved?" Carla asked. "Do you think that was Omar after me in Texas?"

"The name on the driver's license from his billfold didn't say, Omar. But who knows? We'll probably never know." Jack observed her face for several seconds. "Carla, you used some language in a Middle East story you wrote. The terrorists may have interpreted your words as meaning you knew something, that you were more than a journalist. A spy, maybe."

"What? What language are you talking about? Who told you that?"

"An Israeli Mossad agent, Chaim Cohen, told us. You used the words art, key and money together in the same sentence. They referred to Mom as their 'key to the art, to money.' The code name they gave her was in French—*l'argent cle*—key money."

"Jack! I remember that line! But those were not my words. Someone at *World News* inserted them into my story! Were they setting me up? Then they pulled me home from the Middle East and dispatched me to Lawson Preserve. Were they using me? But how? Why? What did they expect me to do here besides write about you and hog hunting? Did they expect me to discover the art?"

"Where's your phone?" Jack asked.

"In my room. Why?"

"Good. We need to tell Macon. Your phone may be bugged."

"What? Why Macon?"

"He's a security contractor working for us ... or for the Israelis. I'm not even sure. But I trust him. His guys took out four men who came here just days ago to kill us. It was a surprise attack at night from the river. Macon's men surprised them. It looks to us like the *World News* used you to write a story that created a protest—a protest meant to serve as a diversion for terrorists intending to attack our family. When that protest failed to achieve results, assassins were dispatched to get the job done."

"What?"

"Believe it or not, I've been preoccupied—one of the reasons I didn't return your calls."

"Wow. I had no idea all of this was going on. And the horrible news coverage on top of it all. I don't blame you."

"Maybe things will settle down. The Israelis have advertised that they've recovered the art. What else could they possibly want from us?"

"That would be nice. I'm ready for a change. No more Caddo Lake ordeals for me!"

Jack smiled like a boy with a secret. "Change is temporary. What we need is transformation. Transformation is permanent."

She smiled back at him, removed her sunglasses and squinted into his eyes. "I'm not sure what that means. But I'm game if you are."

He pulled her close and kissed her.

Mary Catherine stood by the window watching Jack and Carla together in the distance and pondering the lost years.

Albert approached from behind and put his arms around her. "Suzanna and Oliver are in the kitchen. Suzanna can't stop crying. They can't wait to see you."

"Jack and Carla. Where are they in their relationship? Just friends? Or is there something more?"

"I'm not really sure," Albert replied. "Just hopeful." He kissed her temple and they embraced.

"Then so am I."

CHAPTER TWENTY-SIX

A small, unmarked box truck stopped along a deserted stretch of road. It backed up a dirt trail into a pine thicket on Lawson Preserve. Two men got out and lowered a ramp. One man scanned the woods while the other monitored a small device. A rhinoceros-size hog appeared on the trail forty yards north and trotted toward them. It slowed to a walk ten feet shy of the truck, then advanced up the ramp and into the truck's box. The men followed in behind the creature. A minute later, the men descended the ramp and shoved it back in place. They secured the door, climbed into the cab and eased away.

Noonday sun mitigated the chill of crisp, cool air. Jack and Macon sat on the pool deck beneath an umbrella. Macon reclined at ease in pilot sunglasses, a loose V-neck sweater, and jeans. He focused like a soldier, observing Jack as one warrior would observe another during the planning of a serious operation.

Macon's phone rang. He placed it against his ear, still looking at Jack. "Is that right? How interesting. Thanks."

Macon placed his phone on the small table beside him. "Breaking news."

"What now?"

"A camp visitor has mysteriously vanished from Caddo Lake State Park ... without a trace. The local media's reporting his disappearance as an alien abduction. Rangers are combing the park."

Jack smiled. "They'll need to comb some gators if they want to find that dude."

"Yeah. Interesting that his driver's license was issued in Detroit just last month," Macon replied. "And disturbing that he had photos of Carla and Dagny."

"But at least we know it wasn't Omar, after all."

"Negative. Just one of his minions. Omar's still out there. I can smell him. He's probably hiding in some large city. Atlanta, perhaps. Waiting for an opportunity. And then to slip away undetected."

"You make him sound like Satan," Jack replied.

"He is Satan, my friend. Of course, he's human. Highly intelligent. He'll take his time. Strike when you least expect. And use his minions to do his bidding. Another sterling characteristic of your former porcine adversary. There are tens of thousands of illegal criminal aliens and other subversive agents in the United States, thanks to years of a porous border and lax enforcement. Omar's type has been here for years. Americans are oblivious to the threat of terrorism until, like your family, they become targets ... or victims. We need human-intel ASAP. Can you talk with your mother? She's a primary source," Macon said.

"Dad won't allow it. Not yet, anyway. I'm not sure what she's disclosed to him about her experience in captivity or about Omar. I'll ask Dad. But I suspect ..." Jack stopped short of verbalizing his thought. "Our ordeal should be over. But maybe not? Is that what you're saying? Chaim said they'd lose interest in us now that they believe the Israelis have the art."

Macon didn't reply but stared at Jack.

"I can see you disagree. The bodies. Have they been identified?" Jack asked.

"Syrians. Illegals. That's it for now."

"Omar's guys?"

"I would assume."

"On Lawson soil ..."

"That's right. And more where they came from. Social media makes Americans—men, women, children—easy marks for Dark State operatives. Researching and tracking targets has never been easier. Look how fast we located Carla. Terrorist agents are sitting in cages waiting for their masters to snap the release and turn them loose."

"Inferior catch dogs have always gotten on my nerves," Jack said.

Macon laughed. "Mine, too, brother."

"When are you guys pulling out of Lawson Preserve?" Jack asked.

"We can hang out for another day or two unless we have an emergency. After that ..."

"We're on our own?"

"Yeah. We can provide ongoing security. But it'll be expensive."

"What about Carla?"

Macon intertwined his fingers and cracked his knuckles. Instead of answering Jack's question, he flexed his index fingers and thumbs as if shrugging. But he remained silent.

"Carla thinks there may be a clandestine connection between the *World News* and Omar's terrorist cell. That her writing assignment here was a setup. That the media was working some kind of angle in league with Omar, using her as a pawn." Jack paused, waiting for Macon to react. But he wore a poker-face. "She thinks they—whoever they are—may have used her to get info from me about the art. She may be bugged. Any thoughts?"

Macon took a deep breath. "Big bucks attract lots of players. Anything's possible. We can scan her for bugs. But protecting her once she leaves here is another thing altogether. Her safety depends on whether or not they think she's worth the trouble. If I were her, I'd be looking for a new job. Something covert. Until the smoke clears."

Suzanna threw open the back door, yelling, "Lunch is ready."

Jack turned and waved to Suzanna. "Coming." He turned back to Macon. "Let's scan her right away. I'll have a heart-to-heart with Dad. I'm going to lobby for hiring you. I want Omar."

The family sat at the long formal dining table and grinned at each other. Big O and Suzanna joined them, as did Macon and Carla.

"Suzanna, this is a beautiful table and amazing feast. Thank you!" Albert said.

Suzanna beamed. "It's a celebration meal for all the people I love. My great pleasure."

Jack sat between his mother and Carla. He observed Carla, then, with equal admiration, his mother.

Mary Catherine turned to him and smiled. "Your father tells me you play the piano so well."

Jack smiled at his mother. "I've taken a renewed interest in piano lately. I'm okay at it."

Carla rolled her eyes. "He's amazing."

Mary Catherine received Jack's steady gaze—perhaps his very thoughts. She took his hand in hers. As if on cue, everyone joined hands.

"Let's pray," Albert said. They bowed their heads. "Gracious Father, thank you for the many blessings you have bestowed upon this family. Thank you for our friends,

Carla and Macon. And thank you, Lord, for working all things together for good for those who love you and are called according to your purpose. And thank you for this food. Bless it to our bodies and our bodies to your service ..."

Mary Catherine gave Albert's hand a little tug. "Remember Chaim and Israel."

Albert winked approval. "Yes. And Lord, we pray a special blessing upon our friend, Chaim. And the State of Israel. Amen."

Afterward, Suzanna chased everyone from the dining room and kitchen. She and Big O cleared the table and cleaned up. Dagny led Mary Catherine and Carla off to her room for show and tell. Macon eased off to confer with his men at their stations on the Lawson property. Jack and Albert strolled along the river.

"Dad, I think we need to hire Macon's services and keep him around for a while, until we have a clear resolution of things. Omar may still be out there with his people. They know how to find us. They've assaulted us once already. What if they hit us again?"

"Has Macon been able to discern who the attackers were?" Albert asked.

"He said they were Syrians. That's all he knows."

"But we don't know for sure whether Omar was a party to it?"

"No, sir. I guess not. Not yet."

"It would be nice to have security. Of course, we can't afford them forever. At some point, we'll need to work out our own security measures. Perhaps Macon can consult with us about how to manage that."

"Yes, sir," Jack replied. "But I think the best defense is a good offense. I'd like to track Omar and make sure he never hurts our family again."

"You may be out of your league, Jack. Omar's not a hog. He's a man. We best leave him to those who know how to hunt men. Omar's people really have no beef with us now.

They gambled and lost. The Israelis have the art. That fact has been well advertised. Their fight is with others—a fight that's been ongoing for over a thousand years. They'll likely move on."

"As far as I'm concerned, their fight is with me," Jack said.

Albert didn't speak for a few steps. He paused from walking and faced Jack. "Your mother told me everything about Paris. It's not all pretty, Jack. I'll tell you this much: Thanks to Omar, she's alive. For that I'm grateful. God is in control. He works in mysterious ways. He's given us our lives back. We plan to make the best of the years we have left. You need to do the same. Of course, this doesn't mean we ignore burdens and shy away from action. But the choices you make now are crucial to your future. You're young. Strong. Smart. You have the rest of your life. You've been hard on yourself for all these years. It's time to choose a different path. To go forward, not backward."

They exchanged brief smiles. But Jack gritted his teeth, closed his hands into fists, and stared downstream.

Albert pointed to a limb poking from the river. "See that stick?"

Jack nodded. "Yes, sir."

"As we walk along the river's edge, everything about that stick will change. The shifting of the sun's direction will alter its color. And while it appears straight from our present perspective, as we walk along, we may perceive that it's bent. The current flowing against it may affect its position or even suck it under. By the time we pass it, and look back, we may think it's not a stick at all. But some other object. It may even be gone. That's the way life is, Jack. As we walk through life, our perspective on everything changes. We have one perspective when we're young bucks. Another, when we get married. Another, when we become parents. Another, when we lose a loved one. Another, when we go off to war, like Pop. Another, when life sucks us under. In no solitary scene of life do we comprehend its total nature. Not until the end.

"This world is long on lies and short on truth. You, of all people, should know this. You've been stuck in one perspective for a long, long time, Jack. And it may be difficult for you to break out and move on. But if you don't, you may wake up one day and realize you're still stuck in the muck of the river of life, but life has passed you by."

Jack lowered his head. "If only Pop had never brought that art home."

Albert nodded. "Pop took what wasn't his and hid it at Brynhild. That art became a curse. Instead of blessing us, the earth opened up and swallowed us. The curse of feral hogs descended upon us and our community. But we've returned the art and the curse has been lifted. I know it's gone. You, Jack, more than any of us, have carried the burden of Pop's error. It's time you live life free from the curse. Go live your life, Son. Don't blame Pop. Don't hate Omar. Live and love for a change." Albert motioned toward the house. "Back there, I believe there's a young lady who may have an interest in sharing the future with you. None of my business. Just saying ..."

They turned and strolled toward the house without speaking. At the river's bend, they paused again. Jack looked down at his scarred arms and calloused knuckles. He looked at the river, searching for the stick his father had pointed out. It was gone."

He looked Albert in the eyes and nodded. "Thanks, Dad. I get it. I understand God's in control, and I need a new perspective. I'll go live my life. But not blindly, like others—as if evil no longer exists. It does. And as long as it does, I'll be its mortal enemy."

Carla met them at the steps and took Jack's hand. "My turn." She smiled and led him away.

They strolled behind the house, pausing at Amos's grave. Jack stooped down and replaced a stone that had rolled from atop the mound. They strolled farther, stopping at the edge of the woods. A breeze conveyed the aromatic scent of cedars. Jack took a deep breath.

"Ah, smell that?"

"I do. It's wonderful. But cedar, not pine like by the swamp."

Jack smiled. "You remember the smell of the pines by the swamp?"

"A tense visit." She smiled. "But yes. I remember that sweet smell."

"I'm impressed. And encouraged, too," he said.

"Encouraged?"

"Yep."

Carla leaned against a large oak and observed Jack. Sunlight crept through the leaves and danced on her hair. He placed a hand against the tree and returned her gaze.

"How are you, Jack?"

"I'm good."

She raised her eyebrows. "Why am I skeptical?"

"I've been drinking life through a fire hydrant. I guess we all have. But, really, I'm good. I understand things that I've never understood before. I'd like to move on ... one day at a time. I guess ... I've been like one who has believed ... but not surrendered."

"Maybe you can start by surrendering your anger to God, Jack."

He nodded. "Yeah. An ugly companion I've nursed for a long time. It'll be a challenge to depart with. But I'm willing to try. Remember the church service?"

"That Sunday at the chapel?"

"Yeah."

"The miracle?"

"Yeah. That's got to be what Reverend Allen saw." Jack looked into the distance. "God showed him ... Mom. I think he saw her in your eyes ... coming back to us."

"My eyes?"

"Yes. Don't you remember how he stared into your eyes?"

196

"I'll never forget!"

"It's like God brought you here to Brynhild as a messenger of light."

"Me? A messenger of light? That's a stretch!"

"Not at all. In your wake came disclosure, followed by a miracle. Do you know what that means?"

"Umm, no. What?"

"That means you're a helpful girl to have around."

She smiled. "So how can I help you, Jack?"

He looked away as if trying to find the right words. Then he smiled at her. "Two things."

"And they are?"

"One. Help me arrange a meeting with your dad. Two. Kiss me." She pushed away from the tree, grabbed his neck, and they kissed with abandon.

POSTSCRIPT

The inspiration for this novel emerged from a piece I wrote for a hunting blog about a fellow named Marty in Georgia. As of this writing, Marty has actually caught over 1,400 feral hogs using dogs and a knife. Some weighed as much as 490 pounds. Here's Marty's story as told to me:

> We got into hogs right off. Three of my dogs and another guy's dog caught a 140-pound boar. We went in and tied him. Meanwhile, we're hearing shotguns all over. They ended up killing eight on that drive. We got the dogs all circled back in and they bayed a hog here and there. One of my dogs bayed two hogs right in front of a guy. He killed both of them with a shotgun. I think they were using buckshot and twelve gauges.

> I never carry a gun.

> We pushed on. Everything was terribly wet. It had been raining forever. We put the dogs back in and were really struggling through a whole lot of water. Now, some guys with us had a pack of hounds. But no bulldog. And had been running them, but they weren't catching any hogs. What they wanted to do was get the big hog up and running, let him cross a dirt road somewhere, put the cur dogs on him

and stop him. In the world of game-bred hunting dogs, all a cur dog means is it's not a bulldog and it's not a hound dog. In the old school, when they fought dogs, any dog that's not a game-bred dog would cur out.

But when you shoot those cur dogs to the hog, they're fresh and fast. They get ahead of him. And he gets slam worn out. He just can't stand it. And he'll bay up (stop). At this point the hog admits, Okay guys, I can't outrun you and you can't whip me, so I'm gonna stand here and knock your block off. The dogs just stand back then and bark at him—sort a' like treeing a coon or a bear. They're very dangerous at this point. Now sometimes this happens like a textbook and sometimes it just doesn't turn out! This time was textbook.

We stopped on a dirt road. They were looking on the GPS and said, "Here he comes!" We literally didn't sit there three or four minutes before a big black hog crossed the road. We shot our cur dogs to him. I shot two of mine to him. Big O shot a couple to him. They ran him 370 yards from there and bayed him. When they bayed him, I left the dirt road and took off in a sprint running through this old clear-cut. The briars were thick and knee-deep water was almost everywhere. I started to him and yelled for them to send in the bulldogs.

It took me several minutes to get there because it was real thick stuff. I knew where the dogs were from fifty yards away, because I could see the high bushes and little maple trees and whatnot being shaken by the hog fighting the dogs. When I got there, I kicked toward the bushes. I could see the bushes were shaking and I could make out the hog but couldn't tell anything about him. So, I stomped my boot through and tore the underbrush where I could see him. And he was big!

Now, I saw him when he crossed the road, but sometimes from a distance size can be misleading. Anyway, I knew he was big. We had eight or nine dogs baying this hog. We usually don't use that many. But in this situation, we did. Talking about music. They were sounding off. It was good. The hog was doing what we call a rally—haw, haw, haw, haw, haw—gruntin' like that. The dogs were barking and all heck was breakin' loose, limbs poppin' and crackin', the hog popping his teeth together. It was pretty intense. I forget sometimes just how intense—I do this so often. It's an adrenaline rush like no other.

All the dogs were still baying. I maneuvered in behind him. You don't ever want to get in front of a hog. You have to approach him from behind. A lot of people are under the impression that the bulldog, that catch-dog, can hold him down. He's got the hog by the ear—often a dog on each ear. But these dogs are pretty much earrings, holding on for dear life. When I got there, there was a dog on each ear. If you're in front of him, he can shake those bulldogs off and run at you. When I kicked the hole in the briars, I could see his tail was right at me. So, I just reached through and grabbed him by the tail. As soon as I got him by the tail and lifted his back feet off the ground—he drives and spins with those back feet—he stopped fighting the bulldogs. That's when you save those bulldog's lives, because he'll stop fighting them and just start walking forward, generally speaking.

I hollered, "Come on, boys!" When we do that— holler "come on, boys"—they know to holler back because that tells me how far away they are. I don't want to try to throw this hog and nobody closer than two hundred yards of me. Because once you expend the effort to throw him, usually, it's a one-shot thing. Either you get him thrown or it's wasted energy. So, I hollered. Big O was maybe twenty yards and he hollered back. When I heard him holler, I knew he was right there, so I went ahead and attempted to throw him. I stepped under one of his back legs and reached underneath him with my right hand, caught his front leg, threw him and straddled him. As long as I had that front leg, he raised Cain but he couldn't get up. It ain't the easiest thing you've ever done.

Big O, Luke, and somebody else came through the bushes and held him. I tied him up. Sometimes I use mule tape. Sometimes I use handcuffs. We loaded him on the four-wheeler and hauled him out. He had a huge tooth, three and a quarter inches on the right side. The other one was broken at an inch and a half, inch and a quarter, and growing back. Several of the dogs got cut pretty bad. None of mine did.

We always bet on the weight. The closest anyone guessed was 271 pounds. A hog over 250 is a monster. A hog over 300 is really a monster—I don't care what anyone says. This one weighed in at 322!

My wife hunts with me ... occasionally. On one hunt, she was trying to pull a bulldog off a 175-pound boar when the dog let the hog go and caught her in the thigh. He was shaking her. I had to let the hog go to get the dog off my wife. She's a little bitty woman. It was an inferior catch-dog. (Marty laughed.) They caught the hog again later.

I was further influenced by the obvious and growing bias of the global media complex. We are bombarded daily with one view and outright lies on every aspect of life on this planet. And we must apologize for violating the slightest infraction of political correctness ... or else.

Some are more susceptible to propaganda than others. Children, college students, and the chronically uninformed, those who either haven't started thinking yet or have ceased thinking altogether, those who have been taught what to think, not how to think—a primer for totalitarian rule.

It has been alleged that "the news" is controlled by six corporations. Google, at this writing, allegedly influences the thinking of two billion people, a number that is expected to double soon. It has been further alleged that certain US tech companies are cooperating with the Orwellian communist dictators of China. But these same companies have allegedly refused to cooperate with the US military.

Will the masters of deceit ever stop deceiving? Will human freedom survive without the antidote of truth?

"My people are destroyed for lack of knowledge." (Hosea 4:6 NAS)

Lord, open our eyes and expose the lies. Amen.

ABOUT THE AUTHOR

Travel editor for BOOM! Magazine, Barganier also has thirty-five-years' experience in law practice, banking, investments and general business. He's a veteran of the US Army where he graduated from the United States Military Academy Preparatory School, attended West Point, graduated from the Army Signal School and the Savannah River Area Police Academy. He earned a BA in History/Business from Auburn University, and a JD from Jones Law Institute. His publications include a novel, The Slash Brokers (1998), a children's book, The Crooked Tree (2008), and a memoir, How Prayer Helped Me Escape the Corporate Rat Race (2018).

His feature stories on a variety of topics have been published domestically and internationally. Notably, he visited Holland in 2008 and published a feature story in

Dutch the magazine on the history and ancient art of roof thatching. Travel features appear at www.jeffbarganier. com.

He has co-owned and managed Cindy E. Barganier Interiors LLC since 2004, and helped establish Cindy Barganier Textiles Division in 2012. See: www. cindybarganier.com. He and his wife, Cindy, live in Pike Road, Alabama.